THE ART OF PURRING

THE ART OF PURRING

DAVID MICHIE

HAY HOUSE

Carlsbad, California • New York City
London • Sydney • New Delhi

First published and distributed in the United Kingdom by:
Hay House UK Ltd, The Sixth Floor, Watson House,
54 Baker Street, London W1U 7BU
Tel: +44 (0)20 3927 7290; Fax: +44 (0)20 3927 7291; www.hayhouse.co.uk

Published and distributed in the United States of America by:
Hay House Inc., PO Box 5100, Carlsbad, CA 92018-5100
Tel: (1) 760 431 7695 or (800) 654 5126
Fax: (1) 760 431 6948 or (800) 650 5115
www.hayhouse.com

Published and distributed in Australia by:
Hay House Australia Ltd, 18/36 Ralph St, Alexandria NSW 2015
Tel: (61) 2 9669 4299; Fax: (61) 2 9669 4144
www.hayhouse.com.au

Published and distributed in India by:
Hay House Publishers India, Muskaan Complex, Plot No.3, B-2,
Vasant Kunj, New Delhi 110 070
Tel: (91) 11 4176 1620; Fax: (91) 11 4176 1630
www.hayhouse.co.in

Cover design: Amy Rose Grigoriou • *Interior design:* Pamela Homan

To err is human, to purr feline.

ROBERT BYRNE, AUTHOR

PROLOGUE

Oh good, you're finally here, though you've taken your time about it, if you don't mind my saying so! You see, dear reader, I have a message for you. Not an everyday message and certainly not one from an ordinary person. What's more, it concerns your deepest, personal happiness.

There's really no need to turn around to see who may be standing behind you or, indeed, to either side. This message really is for *you*.

It's not everyone in the world who gets to read these words—only a very tiny minority of humans ever will. Nor should you believe that it's some kind of chance event that finds you reading them at this particular moment in your life. Only those of you with very specific karma will ever discover what I'm about to say—readers with a particular connection to me.

Or should I say *us*.

You see, I am the Dalai Lama's Cat, and the message I have for you comes from none other than His Holiness.

How can I make such a preposterous claim? Have I taken complete leave of my senses? If you will allow me to curl up on your metaphorical lap I will explain.

At some point, nearly every cat lover faces a dilemma: How do you tell your feline companion that you are going away? And not just for a long weekend.

Exactly *how* humans break the news of their impending absence is a subject of great concern to cats. Some of us like plenty of advance warning so we can mentally steel ourselves for the change in routine. Others prefer the news to swoop unheralded from the sky like an angry magpie in nesting season: by the time you realize what's about to happen, it already has.

Interestingly, our staff members seem to have an innate sense of this and act accordingly, some sweet-talking their puss for weeks before their departure, others producing the dreaded cat carrier from the storage cupboard without notice.

As it happens, I am among the most fortunate of cats, because when the Dalai Lama goes traveling, the household routine here at Namgyal continues in much the same way. I still spend part of each day on his first-floor windowsill, a vantage point from which I can maintain maximum surveillance with minimum effort, just as I spend some time most days in the office of His Holiness's executive assistants. And then there is my regular stroll a short distance away to the congenial surroundings and delectable enticements of the Himalaya Book Café.

Even so, when His Holiness isn't here life is not the same. How can I describe what it is like to be in the presence of the Dalai Lama? Quite simply, it is extraordinary. From the moment he enters a room, every being within it is touched by his energy of heartfelt happiness. Whatever else may be going on in your life, whatever tragedy or loss you may be facing, for the time that you are with His Holiness, you experience the sensation that deep down all is well.

If you haven't experienced this before, it is like being awakened to a dimension of yourself that has been there all this time, flowing like an underground river although until now it has gone undetected. Reconnected to this source, you not only experience the profound peace and wellspring at the heart of your being, but you may also, for a moment, catch a glimpse of your own conscious-ness—radiant, boundless, and imbued with love.

The Dalai Lama sees us as we really are and reflects our true nature back to us. This is why so many people simply melt in his presence. I've seen important men in dark suits cry just because he touched them on the arm. Leaders of the world's great religions line up to meet him and then rejoin the line to be introduced to him a second time. I've watched people in wheelchairs weep tears of joy when he went four deep into a crowd to take their hand. His Holiness reminds us of the best that we can be. Is there a greater gift?

So you will understand, dear reader, that even though I continue to enjoy a life of privilege and comfort when the Dalai Lama is traveling, I still very much prefer it when he is at home. His Holiness knows this, just as he recognizes that I am a cat who likes to be told when he is going away. If either of his executive assistants—young Chogyal, the roly-poly monk who helps him with monas-tic matters, or Tenzin, the seasoned diplomat who helps him in secular business—presents him with a request involving travel, he will look up and say something like, "Two days in New Delhi at the end of next week."

They may think he is confirming the visit. In reality, he is saying this specifically for *my* benefit.

In the days leading up to a longer journey, he will remind me of the trip by visualizing the number of sleeps—that is, nights—he will be away. And on the final evening before his departure, he always makes sure we have some quality time alone together, just the two of us. In these few minutes we commune in the profound way possible only between cats and their human companions.

Which brings me back to the message His Holiness asked me to pass on to you. He brought it up the evening before his departure on a seven-week teaching trip to the United States and Europe—the longest time we had ever been apart. As twilight fell over Kangra Valley, he pushed back from his desk, walked over to where I was resting on the sill, and kneeled beside me. "I have to go tomorrow, my little Snow Lion," he said, looking deep into my blue eyes as he used his favorite term of endearment. It's one that delights me, as the Tibetans consider snow lions to be celestial beings, symbolizing beauty, fearlessness, and cheerfulness. "Seven weeks is longer than I am usually away. I know you like me to be here, but there are other beings who need me, too."

I got up from where I was resting and, placing my paws out in front of me, had a good, long stretch before yawning widely.

"What a nice, pink mouth," His Holiness said, smiling. "I am glad to see your teeth and gums in good condition."

Moving closer, I affectionately head-butted him.

"Oh, you make me laugh!" he said. We remained there, forehead to forehead, as he ran his fingers down my neck. "I am going away for some time, but your happiness should not depend on me being here. You can still be very happy."

With his fingertips he massaged the back of my ears, just the way I like.

"Perhaps you think happiness comes from being with me or from the food you are given down at the café." His Holiness had no illusions about why I was such an eager patron of the Himalaya Book Café. "But over the next seven weeks, try to discover for yourself the *true* cause of happiness. When I get back, you can tell me what you have found."

Gently and with deep affection, the Dalai Lama took me in his arms and stood facing the open window and the view down Kangra Valley. It was a magnificent sight: the verdant, winding valley, the rolling evergreen forests. In the distance, the icy summits of the Himalayas gleamed in the late afternoon sunshine. The gentle breeze wafting through the window was redolent of pine, rhododendron, and oak; the air stirred with enchantment.

"I will tell you the true causes of happiness," he whispered in my ear. "A special message just for you—and for those with whom you have a karmic connection."

I began to purr, and soon my purring rose to the steady, throaty volume of a miniature outboard motor. "Yes, my little Snow Lion," the Dalai Lama said. "I would like you to investigate the art of purring."

CHAPTER ONE

Have you ever marveled, dear reader, at how the most apparently trivial decision can sometimes lead to the most life-changing events? You make what you believe to be a humdrum, everyday kind of choice, and it has outcomes as dramatic as they are unforeseen.

That is exactly what happened the Monday afternoon I decided that instead of going straight home from the Himalaya Book Café, I would take the so-called scenic path. It was not a route I had taken very often, for the simple reason that it isn't really very scenic—or even much of a path. It is more of a humble back alley that runs along behind the Himalaya Book Café and the adjacent premises.

It is, however, a longer way home, so I knew it would take me ten minutes rather than the usual five to get back to Namgyal. But having spent the afternoon asleep on the magazine rack of the café, I felt the need to stretch my legs.

So when I reached the front door, instead of turning right, I headed left. Ambling past the side doors of the café I made another left turn and walked along the narrow lane used for garbage cans, redolent with kitchen scraps and tantalizing aromas. I continued on my way, somewhat wobbly, as my hind legs have been weak since I was a kitten. I paused once to cuff at an intriguing silver-and-brown object lodged under the rear gate of the café, only to discover that it was a champagne cork that had somehow gotten jammed in the grill.

It was as I was preparing to turn left again that I first became aware of danger. About 20 yards away, on the main street, I spotted a pair of the largest and most ferocious looking dogs I had ever seen. Strangers to the district, they were a menacing presence as they stood with nostrils flared and long fur rippling in the late afternoon breeze.

Worst of all, they were unleashed.

With the wisdom of hindsight, what I should have done at that point was retreat back into the alley and exit through the café's rear gate, where I would have been completely secure behind bars wide enough for me to slip through but much too narrow for these monsters.

In the exact moment I was wondering if they had seen me, they saw me and instantly gave chase. Instinct kicking in, I made a sharp right and scrambled as fast as my uncertain limbs would take me. Heart pounding and hair standing on end, I raced desperately in search of refuge. For those few adrenaline-charged moments I felt capable of going anywhere and doing anything, be it scrambling up the tallest tree or squeezing through the narrowest gap.

But there was no escape route, no safe ground. The dogs' vicious baying was getting louder as they closed in behind me. In an absolute panic, with nowhere else to turn, I darted into a spice shop, thinking that I might find some place to climb to safety or at least be able to throw the dogs off my scent.

The tiny shop was lined with wooden chests on which brass bowls of spices were carefully laid out. Several matronly women, who were grinding powder in pestles on their laps, let out cries of shock as I ran past their ankles, followed by bellows of outrage as the dogs, high on bloodlust, bounded after me.

I heard a crash of metal on concrete as bowls tumbled. Clouds of spices exploded into the air. Racing to the back of the store, I looked for a shelf to jump up on but found only a firmly closed door. However, there was a gap between two chests that was just wide enough for me to claw my way through. Behind it, in place of a wall, there was only a torn plastic sheet and, beyond that, a deserted lane.

Shoving their great heads into the gap between the chests, the dogs launched into a frenzy of yapping. Terrified, I quickly scanned the gutter: it came to a dead end. The only way out would be to go back to the road.

From inside the spice store came plaintive yelping as the angry women apprehended the two thugs. With my usually lustrous white coat dusted with spices of every color, I scampered along the gutter to the road and ran as fast as my frail legs would take me. But the road was on an incline, slight but punishing. Even though I was straining every sinew of my being, my efforts were to little avail. Struggling to get as far away from the dogs as I could, I searched for somewhere, anywhere, that offered protection. But I saw only shop windows, concrete walls, and impenetrable steel gates.

Behind me the commotion of barking continued, now accompanied by the angry yelling of the women from the spice shop. I turned to see them shoving the dogs out of the shop, slapping them on the flanks. Wild-eyed and with tongues hanging out, the two slavering beasts pawed the pavement outside, while I continued struggling uphill, hoping the steady stream of pedestrians and cars would conceal my whereabouts.

But there was to be no escape.

Within moments the two beasts had caught my scent and resumed the chase. Their ferocious growling filled me with pure fear.

I had gained some ground, but it wasn't enough. It would take hardly any time for the two beasts to catch up. Reaching a property surrounded by high white walls, I spotted a wooden trellis climbing one wall, next to a black iron gate. Never before would I have even considered what I did next, but what choice did I have? With only seconds before the dogs would be upon me, I leapt onto the trellis and began scrambling up it as fast as my fluffy gray legs would let me. With great lurches I dragged myself up, paw by paw.

I had just reached the top when the beasts closed in. Amid a frenzy of barking, they hurled themselves against the trellis. There was a crash of wood as the lattice cracked, and the top half swung away from the wall. Had I still been scaling it, I would have found myself dangling over the dogs' gaping maws.

Standing on top of the wall, I looked down at their bared teeth and trembled at their blood-curdling snarls. It was like looking directly into the faces of beings from the hell realms.

The manic frenzy of noise continued until the dogs

were distracted by a canine licking something off the pavement farther down the street. As they raced toward that dog, the beasts were stopped short by a tall man in a tweed jacket, who seized them by the collar and snapped on their leashes. As he was bending over them, I heard a passerby remark, "Beautiful Labradors!"

"Golden retrievers," corrected the man. "Young and high-spirited. But," he added, patting them affectionately, "lovely animals."

Lovely animals? Had the whole world gone totally mad?

It was ages before my heart rate returned to something approaching normal, and only then was the reality of my situation apparent. Looking around, I could find no branch or ledge or escape route of any kind. The wall on which I was standing had a gate at one end and a sheer drop at the other. I was about to raise paw to mouth to give my spice-smeared face a much-needed and reassuring wash when I caught a whiff of something so pungent that it made me stop instantly. Just one lick, I knew, would set my mouth on fire. That did it. There I was, trapped on a high and unfamiliar wall, and I couldn't even groom myself!

I had no choice but to stay where I was and wait for something to happen. In stark contrast to all the turmoil I was feeling, the property inside the wall was the very picture of serenity, like the Pure Lands of the Buddhas that I had heard the monks talking about. Through the trees I could see a large, stately building surrounded by rolling lawns and flower-filled gardens. I longed to be down in those gardens or prowling along the veranda—it looked like just the kind of place where I would fit in. If someone inside that beautiful building spotted the snow lion stranded on top of their wall, surely they would have the compassion to come to my rescue?

But despite much activity at the main gate of the building, no one walked in or out of the pedestrian gate near me. And the wall was so high that passersby on the sidewalk could barely see me. The few who did glance my way seemed to take no notice. As time went by and the sun began to slide toward the horizon, I realized that I would be there all night if no one came to my aid. I let out a meow that was plaintive but restrained: I knew only too well that many people don't like cats and coming to their attention would only put me in an even worse predicament.

I needn't have worried about unwanted attention, however, because I received no attention at all. In the Himalaya Book Café I might be revered as HHC, the Dalai Lama's Cat. But out here, spice-stained and unknown, I was completely ignored.

Dear reader, I will spare you a full account of the next few hours I spent on the wall and the indifferent glances and uncomprehending smiles I was forced to endure, along with the stones thrown by two bored scamps on their way home from school. It was after nightfall and I was weary with fatigue when I noticed a woman walking along across the street. At first I didn't recognize her, but there was something about her that gave me a sense that she would be the one to save me.

I meowed imploringly. She crossed the road. As she drew closer I saw that it was Serena Trinci, the daughter of Mrs. Trinci, His Holiness's VIP chef and my most ardent admirer at Namgyal. Recently appointed caretaker-manager of the Himalaya Book Café, Serena was in her mid-30s. Looking svelte, her dark shoulder-length hair gathered in a ponytail, she was dressed in her yoga clothes.

"Rinpoche!" she exclaimed, looking aghast. "What are you doing up there?"

We had seen each other only twice at the café, so when she recognized me, my relief was beyond measure. Within moments she had dragged a nearby garbage can over to the wall and climbed up to where I was. Gathering me in her arms, she couldn't help noticing the bedraggled state of my spice-flecked coat.

"What's happened, poor little thing?" she asked, taking in the multicolored stains and pungent aromas as she held me close. "You must have been in some sort of trouble."

Nuzzling my face into her chest, I felt enveloped by the warm fragrance of her skin and the reassuring beat of her heart. Step by step, as we made our way home, my relief deepened into something altogether stronger: a powerful sense of connection.

Having spent most of her adult life in Europe, Serena had arrived back in McLeod Ganj—the part of Dharamsala where the Dalai Lama lives—only a few weeks earlier. She had grown up there, in a household devoted to food. So after high school she had gone to catering college in Italy and then worked as a chef, rising through the ranks at some of Europe's best restaurants.

Recently she had left her post as head chef at Venice's iconic Hotel Danieli for the top job at a fashionable restaurant in Mayfair, an upscale part of London.

I knew that Serena was ambitious, energetic, and extremely gifted, and I had heard her explain to Franc, owner of the Himalaya Book Café, how she had felt the need for a break from the 24-hour treadmill of restaurant life. She was burned out from the relentless stress, and it was time to rest and recharge: when she returned to London in six months, she would be taking on one of the most prestigious jobs in the city.

Little had she known that her arrival home would coincide with the exact moment that Franc needed someone to look after the café. He was returning to San Francisco to take care of his father, who was seriously ill. While managing any kind of food business hadn't figured in Serena's holiday plans, compared to what she was used to, taking care of the Himalaya Book Café would seem like a part-time job. The café was open for dinner only from Thursday through Saturday; and with the head waiter, Kusali, overseeing daytime service, the demands on Serena would not be great. It would be fun, Franc assured her, and give her something to do.

More important, he needed someone to take care of his two dogs. Marcel, the French bulldog, and Kyi Kyi, the Lhasa Apso, were the other two nonhuman habitués of the café, dozing through most of the day in their wicker basket under the reception counter.

Within two weeks Serena's presence at the café had made its mark; on meeting her, people immediately fell under her spell. Patrons of the café couldn't help but respond to her vivacity: she seemed to know just how to turn an evening out into a night to remember. As she breezed through the café, her warmth and upbeat personality soon had the waiters falling all over themselves to please her. Sam, the bookstore manager, was openly captivated by her, and Kusali, tall and shrewd—an Indian Jeeves—took her under his paternal wing.

I had been resting in my usual place—the top shelf of the magazine stand, between *Vogue* and *Vanity Fair*—when Franc introduced me to Serena as *Rinpoche*. Pronounced rin-po-shay, it means *precious one* in Tibetan and is an honorific given to learned Tibetan Buddhist teachers. Serena had responded to the introduction by reaching out and caressing my face. "How utterly adorable!" is all she said.

My lapis-blue eyes had met her gleaming dark ones, and there was a moment of recognition. I became aware of something that is of the utmost importance to cats, something we innately sense: I was in the presence of a cat lover.

Now, in the wake of my run-in with the dogs and the spice shop, Serena, with help from Kusali and some warm, wet cloths, was tenderly wiping away the spices that had become embedded in my thick coat. We were in the restaurant laundry, a small room behind the kitchen.

"Not so nice for Rinpoche," remarked Serena as she removed a dark smudge from one of my gray boots with great delicacy. "But I just love the smell of all these spices. They take me back to our kitchen at home when I was growing up: cinnamon, cumin, cardamom, cloves—the wonderful flavors of garam masala, which we used in chicken curry and other dishes."

"You prepared curries, Miss Serena?" Kusali was surprised.

"That's how I started out in the kitchen," she told him. "Those were the flavors of my childhood. Now Rinpoche is bringing them all back."

"Our esteemed diners are often asking if we have Indian dishes on the menu, ma'am."

"I know. I've had several requests already."

There was no shortage of kiosks, street kitchens, and more formal restaurants in Dharamsala. But as Kusali observed, "People seek a trusted purveyor."

"You're right," agreed Serena. Then, after a pause she added, "But Franc was pretty clear about sticking to the menu."

"And we must respect his wishes"—Kusali was emphatic—"on the nights the café is customarily open."

There was a pause while Serena removed several whole peppercorns that had lodged themselves in my bushy tail and Kusali dabbed tentatively at a garish splash of paprika on my chest.

When Serena spoke next there was a smile in her voice. "Kusali, are you saying what I think you're saying?"

"Sorry, ma'am, I am not understanding."

"Are you thinking we might open on a Wednesday, say, to try out a few curry dishes?"

Kusali met her eyes with an expression of wonderment and a broad smile. "A most excellent idea, ma'am!"

We cats have no fondness for water, and a damp cat is an unhappy one. Serena knew this, so as soon as she and Kusali had cleaned my coat to something approaching its usual pristine condition, she dried me with a towel chosen especially for its fluffiness, before asking Kusali to find a few morsels of chicken breast to tide me over until she took me home to Jokhang.

Being a Monday evening, the restaurant was closed, but Kusali found some delectable morsels in the fridge and warmed them briefly before placing them in the small china bowl kept exclusively for me. From force of habit, he took it to my usual spot at the back of the café, and Serena followed with me in her arms.

Although the café was in semidarkness, it so happened that Sam Goldberg, the bookstore manager, was hosting a book club meeting that night. Leaving me to my dinner, which I attacked with gusto, Serena and Kusali went to the bookstore section of the café, where 20 or so people were sitting on chairs set up in rows, watching a slide presentation.

"This is an illustration of the future from a book written in the late 1950s," a male voice was saying. The speaker's shaven head, wire-rimmed spectacles, and goatee gave him a cheeky look, adding to the aura of naughtiness about him. I recognized the face instantly. Sam had hung a poster of him in the store several weeks earlier, along with a quote from *Psychology Today* describing the man—a well-known psychologist—as "one of the foremost thought leaders of our time."

It was then that I noticed Sam standing at the back to greet latecomers. Fresh-faced and handsome, Sam has a high forehead, curly, dark hair, and hazel eyes that, behind his somewhat geeky glasses, convey a luminous intelligence, along with a curious lack of self-confidence. Like Serena, Sam had been working at the Himalayan

Book Café for only a short while, although his was a permanent job.

Sam had established himself as a regular patron at the café several months ago, and when Franc quizzed him about the books and downloads that seemed to hold his constant attention, Sam explained that he had worked in a major Los Angeles bookstore until it had recently closed down. This had instantly grabbed Franc's attention. Franc had been thinking of converting the underused space in Café Franc, as it was known then, into a bookstore, but he needed someone with experience to make it happen. If ever there was a case of right person, right place, right time, this was it.

But it had taken some persuasion. Sam was still nursing his wounds from being laid off when the LA bookstore closed down and didn't think he was up to the job. Franc had had to use all of his charm—aided by the considerable powers of persuasion of his lama, Geshe Wangpo—to get Sam to relent and set up the bookstore section of the Himalaya Book Café.

"Bearing in mind that from a 1950s perspective, today *is* the future," continued Sam's guest speaker, "would anyone care to comment on the accuracy of the author's vision?"

There were chuckles from the audience. The picture on the screen showed a housewife dusting the furniture, while outside her husband was docking his antigravity car, having descended from a sky filled with flying cars and people with jet packs on their backs

"The Lucille Ball hairdo isn't very futuristic," one of the women in the audience remarked, to even more laughter. "The clothes," someone else said to more guffaws. The woman in her puffy skirt and her husband in his drainpipe pants clearly didn't look like anyone we would see today.

"What about those jet packs?" contributed another.

"That's right," agreed the speaker. "We're still waiting for them." He flicked through several more images. "These show what people back in the 1950s thought the future would be like. And what makes these images so wonderfully, charmingly wrong isn't just what's in the pictures. It's also what's *not* in them. Tell me what's missing from this one," he said, pausing at an artist's rendering of a streetscape in 2020, with conveyer belts as sidewalks, whisking pedestrians along.

Absorbed as I was in my chicken dinner, even I found the image on the screen surreal for reasons I couldn't quite place. There was a pause before someone observed, "No mobile phones."

"No female executives," offered another.

"No people of color," said someone.

"No tattoos," added somebody else, as the audience began to notice more and more.

The speaker allowed a few moments for the images to sink in. "You might say that the difference between the way things were in the 1950s and the way people imagined the future to be came down to what they focused on—antigravity cars, say, or conveyer-belted sidewalks. They imagined that everything else would stay the same."

There was a pause while the audience digested what he had just said.

"That, my friends, is one reason why we are all so poor at guessing how we'll feel about certain things in the future—in particular, about what is likely to make us happy. It's because we imagine that everything in our lives will stay just the same except for the one thing that we're focused on.

"Some call this *presentism*, the tendency to think that the future will be just like the present but with one particular difference. Our minds are very good at filling in everything else, apart from that difference, when we think about tomorrow. And the material we use to fill it in with is today as these images illustrate."

Continuing, the speaker said, "Research shows that when we make predictions about how we'll feel about future events, we don't realize that our minds have played this 'filling in' trick. That's part of why we think that getting the job with the corner office will deliver a feeling of success and achievement, or that driving an expensive car will be a source of undiluted joy. We think our lives will be just the same as they are now, with that one point of difference. But the reality, as we've seen"—the speaker gestured toward the screen—"is a lot more complicated. We don't imagine, for example, the huge shift in work-life balance that comes with the corner-office job or the anxiety we'll feel about getting scratches and dents in the shiny new car, not to mention the pain of those monthly lease payments."

I could have stayed longer to listen to the speaker, but Serena wanted to get home, and she was going to see me safely back to Jokhang. Carrying me in her arms, she slipped out the back door of the café and took the short walk up the road. At Namgyal we made our way across the courtyard to His Holiness's residence, where Serena bent down and placed me, like a piece of delicate porcelain, on the steps to the main entrance.

"I hope you're feeling more yourself, little Rinpoche," she murmured, running her fingers through my coat, which was now almost dry. I loved the feel of her long fingernails massaging my skin. Reaching over, I licked her leg with my sandpaper tongue.

She laughed. "Oh, my little girl, I love you, too!"

Chogyal, one of His Holiness's assistants, had left dinner for me upstairs in the usual place, but having already eaten at the café I wasn't really hungry. After lapping up some lactose-free milk, I made my way into the private quarters I shared with His Holiness. The room where he spent most of each day was silent and lighted only by the moon. I headed to my favorite spot on the windowsill. Even though the Dalai Lama was many miles away in America, I felt his presence as if he were right beside me. Perhaps it was the spell of the moonlight, which cast everything in the room in an ethereal monochrome, but whatever the reason, I felt a profound sense of peace. It was the same feeling of well-being I experienced whenever I was with him. I think what he was telling me as he left on his trip was that this flow of serenity and benevolence is something any of us can connect with. We only need to sit quietly.

I began licking my paw and washing my face for the first time since the horrors of the afternoon. I could still see the dogs bearing down on me, but now it felt as though I was picturing events that had happened to some other cat. What had seemed so overwhelming and traumatic at the time diminished to just a memory in the tranquility of Namgyal.

I remembered the psychologist down at the café describing how people often have little idea about what will make them happy. His illustrations were intriguing, and as he spoke, something else struck me about his message: it was quite familiar because the Dalai Lama often used to say the same thing. He didn't use words like *presentism*, but his meaning was identical. His Holiness also observed how we tell ourselves that our happiness depends on certain situations, relationships, or accomplishments. How we think we'll be unhappy if we don't get what we want. Just as he pointed out the paradox that, even when we *do* get what we want, it often fails to deliver the happiness we expect.

Settling down on the sill, I gazed out into the night. Squares of light flickered through the darkness from the monks' residences. Aromas wafted through the first floor window, hinting at the evening meals being prepared in the monastery kitchens. I listened to the bass-toned chants from the temple, as the senior monks brought their early evening meditation session to a close. Despite the trauma of the afternoon and coming back to an empty, unlighted home, as I sat on the sill with my paws tucked under me, I felt a contentment more profound than I would have ever predicted.

The next few days were a buzz of activity down at the Himalaya Book Café. Along with all the usual busyness, Serena was rapidly evolving her ideas for a curry night. She consulted with the café chefs, the Nepalese brothers Jigme and Ngawang Dragpa, who were only too happy to share their own family favorites. She also scoured the Internet for rare treasures to add to her already full recipe book of personal favorites.

One Monday night Serena invited a group of friends she had grown up with in McLeod Ganj to sample some of the curry dishes she had rediscovered or reinvented. From the kitchen came a mélange of enticing spices never before combined in such glorious profusion at the café—coriander and fresh ginger, sweet paprika and hot chili, garam masala, yellow mustard seeds, and nutmeg.

Working in the kitchen for the first time since returning from Europe, Serena was in her element as she prepared crunchy vegetarian samosas, removed generous helpings of naan—Indian flatbread—from the oven, and decorated brass bowls of Madras curry with spirals of yogurt. She remembered the sheer joy of creation, the passion that had led her to train as a professional chef. Experimenting with a whole palette of flavors was something she hadn't ventured in 15 years.

Her friends had been grateful but constructive critics. Such was their enthusiasm that by the time the last pistachio-and-cardamom *kulfi* had been eaten and the last glass of chai had been drunk, the idea of a curry night had expanded into something altogether more extravagant: it was to be an Indian banquet.

I was the top-shelf witness to the inaugural banquet less than two weeks later. As the abiding presence of the Himalaya Book Café, why would I not be? Besides, Serena had promised me a generous serving of her delectable Malabar fish curry.

Never had there been so many diners in the restaurant at one time. The event had proven so popular that extra tables had to be brought into the bookstore area and two additional waitstaff hired for the night. Joining the local residents who were café regulars were Serena's family and friends, many of whom had known Serena as a child. Serena's mother was operatic and center stage in a multicolored Indian shawl, her gold bracelets jangling at her wrists and her amber eyes flashing with pride as she watched her daughter choreograph the evening.

As if to compensate for the Italian brio, at the table next to Mrs. Trinci's was a more sedate contingent from the Dalai Lama's office, including His Holiness's executive assistants, Chogyal and Tenzin, along with Tenzin's wife, Susan, and His Holiness's translator, Lobsang.

Chogyal, with his warm heart and soft hands, was my favorite monk after the Dalai Lama. With wisdom well beyond his years in dealing with often-tricky monastic matters, he was of great assistance to His Holiness. He was also responsible for feeding me when the Dalai Lama was away, a duty he performed punctiliously.

It had been Chogyal who, a year earlier, had volunteered to take me home with him while the Dalai Lama's quarters were being redecorated. After lashing out at him for having the temerity to remove me from all that was familiar, I had spent three days sulking under the bedcovers, only to discover that I had been missing out on an exciting new world, one inhabited by a magnificent tabby who was to become the father of my kittens. Through all these adventures Chogyal had remained my patient and devoted friend.

Across the desk from him in the executive assistants' office sat Tenzin, a suave professional diplomat whose hands always had the tang of carbolic soap about them. He had been educated in Britain, and I had learned most of what I knew about European culture from lunchtimes in the first-aid room, listening to the BBC World Service with Tenzin.

I didn't know Tenzin's wife, Susan, but I was familiar with His Holiness's translator, Lobsang, a deeply serene young monk. Lobsang and Serena had known each other from way back, having both grown up together in McLeod Ganj. A relative of the royal family of Bhutan, Lobsang had been a novice monk studying at Namgyal when Mrs. Trinci needed extra sous-chefs in the kitchen. He and Serena had been conscripted, and a close and delightful friendship had ensued, which was why Lobsang was also present for the Indian banquet.

The night of the banquet, Serena had transformed the café into a sumptuous dining room with richly embroidered and sequined tablecloths on which she had placed exquisitely carved condiment pots. Clustered at every setting were flickering tea lights in brass lotus-flower candle holders.

Indian trance music swelled and ebbed hypnotically in the background as a parade of dishes appeared from the kitchen. From the vegetable *pakoras* to the mango chicken, each one of them received an ecstatic response. As for the Malabar fish curry, I could personally vouch for it. The fish was mild and succulent, the sauce deliciously creamy, with just enough coriander, ginger, and cumin to deliver a delightful zing. Within minutes I not only had eaten my serving but had licked the saucer clean.

At the center of everything, Serena was masterfully in command. She had dressed especially for the performance in a crimson sari, with kohl makeup, chandelier earrings, and a glittering jeweled collar. As the evening wore on, she went from table to table, and I couldn't help but notice how touched people were by her warm heart.

During the time she spent with them, she made them feel as if they were the center of her world. And she in turn was moved by the outpouring of affection she received.

"It's so wonderful that you've come back, my dear," an elderly lady who was a family friend told her. "We love all your ideas and energy."

"We've needed someone like you in Dharamsala," a classmate from Serena's school days had said. "All the most talented people seem to leave, so when someone comes back we treasure them more than you can imagine."

Several times during the evening I watched her lip tremble with emotion as she raised a handkerchief to dab the corner of her eye. Something special was happening in the Himalaya Book Café, something that went beyond the Indian banquet, however sumptuous, and was of much greater personal significance.

The clue to it came several nights later.

Over the past few weeks, an intriguing working relationship had been unfolding between Serena and Sam. Serena's vivacity was the perfect complement to Sam's shyness. His cerebral wonderland was balanced by the here-and-now world of food and wine that she inhabited. And knowing that she was only a caretaker who would be returning to Europe in a few months gave their time together a bittersweet evanescent quality.

They had gotten into the habit of ending each evening that the café was open for dinner in a particular corner of the bookstore section. Two sofas arranged on either side of a coffee table made the perfect spot from which to survey the last of the restaurant's diners and talk about whatever was on their minds.

Headwaiter Kusali no longer needed to be asked to bring their order. Shortly after they sat down, he would arrive bearing a tray with two Belgian hot chocolates, one with marshmallows for Serena, the other with biscotti for Sam. Also on the tray would be a saucer with four dog biscuits and, if I was still at the café, a small jug of lactose-free milk.

The soft *clink* of the saucer on the coffee table was the cue for Marcel and Kyi Kyi, who had obediently remained in their basket under the counter for the whole of dinner service. The two dogs would scramble from their basket, race across the restaurant and up the stairs, before sitting at the coffee table with heads cocked and pleading eyes. Their eagerness never failed to bring a smile to the faces of their two human companions, who would watch the dogs devour their biscuits, snuffling up any crumbs on the floor.

I would make my way over in more leisurely fashion, stretching myself for a few quivering moments before hopping down from the top shelf of the magazine rack to join the others.

After their biscuits, the dogs would jump up on the sofa, flanking Sam as they lay on their backs, in eager anticipation of a tummy rub. I would take my place in Serena's lap, kneading whatever dress she happened to be wearing while giving her an appreciative purr.

"There's already been a flurry of bookings for our next banquet," Serena told Sam that particular evening after all five of us were settled.

"That's great!" he said, sipping his hot chocolate contemplatively. "H-have you decided when you're going to tell Franc?"

Serena hadn't. Still in San Francisco, Franc knew nothing about last Wednesday's Indian banquet experiment. Serena had been holding to the wisdom that it is sometimes better to beg forgiveness than to ask permission.

"I thought I'd let him have a pleasant surprise when he gets the month's financials," she said.

"He'll get a surprise all right," agreed Sam. "The biggest take for a single night since the café opened. And it has turbocharged everything since. The whole place has become more vibrant. There's more of a buzz."

"I've thought that, too," said Serena. "But I wondered if I was the only one."

"No, the place has changed," Sam insisted, holding her eyes for a full two seconds before breaking his gaze. "You've changed, too."

"Oh?" she said, smiling. "How?"

"You've got this . . . energy. This j-joie de v-vivre."

Serena nodded. "I do feel different. I've been thinking about how in all those years of managing some of the most upscale restaurants in Europe, I don't think I ever had as much fun as I did last Wednesday night. I never would have believed it could be so wonderfully satisfying!"

Sam reflected for a moment before observing, "As that psychologist said the other day, sometimes it's hard to predict what will make us happy."

"Exactly. I'm beginning to wonder if being head chef at one of London's top restaurants really *is* what I want to do next."

I was looking at Sam as she said this and observed the change in his expression. A gleam came into his eyes.

"If I go back to doing the same thing," continued Serena, "it will probably produce the same result."

"More stress and b-burnout?"

She nodded. "There are rewards, too, of course. But they're very different from the ones here."

"Do you think it was cooking for family and friends that made the difference?" Sam suggested. Then, flashing a mischievous glance he added, "Or was it about awakening the *vindaloo* within?"

Serena chuckled. "Both. I've always adored curries. Even though they'll never be haute cuisine, I love cooking them because of the many flavors, and they're so nourishing. But as well as that, it felt as if last Wednesday was really special for people."

"I agree," said Sam. "The place had a great vibe."

"There's something very fulfilling when you can do what you really care about, and it's appreciated by others."

Sam looked pensive before putting down his mug, rising from the sofa, and going to a bookshelf. He returned with a paperback copy of *Man's Search for Meaning*, by the Austrian psychologist and Holocaust survivor Viktor Frankl. "What you just said reminded me of something," he said, opening the book at its preface. "'Don't aim at success,'" he read. "'The more you aim at it and make it a target, the more you are going to miss it. For success, like happiness, cannot be pursued; it must ensue . . . as the unintended side effect of one's dedication to a course greater than oneself.'"

Serena nodded. "In a very small way, I think that's what I'm discovering." For a moment they held each other's eyes. "And in the strangest of ways."

Sam was curious. "How do you mean?"

"Well, the whole idea of an Indian banquet only happened because of a chance conversation I had with

Kusali. And *that* only happened because I found little Rinpoche stranded."

Sam knew about the afternoon I had been trapped on the wall. There had been much speculation about how I had ended up there, none of it correct.

"You might say that all of this only came about because of Rinpoche," she said, gazing down adoringly and stroking me.

"Rinpoche, the catalyst," observed Sam.

As the two of them chuckled, I thought how no one, least of all me, could ever have guessed at the chain of events that would be triggered by my decision that Monday afternoon to turn left instead of right when I left the café. Nor would any of us have believed what was still to come. For what had happened so far turned out to be only the beginning of a much bigger story—a story in which many dimensions of happiness were to emerge as unintended but most rewarding side effects.

Unpredictable? Most certainly. Enlightening? Indubitably!

CHAPTER TWO

What makes you purr?

Of all the questions in the world, this is the most important. It is also the great leveler. Because no matter whether you are a playful kitten or a sedentary senior, a scrawny alley Tom or a sleek-coated uptown girl, whatever your circumstances you just want to be happy. Not the kind of happy that comes and goes like a can of flaked tuna, but an enduring happiness. The deep-down happiness that makes you purr from the heart.

Only a few days after the Indian banquet, I made another intriguing discovery about happiness. Midway through a glorious Himalaya morning—blue skies, fluting birdsong, the invigorating scent of pine—I heard unfamiliar sounds coming from the bedroom. Hopping off my sill, I went to investigate.

Chogyal was supervising a spring cleaning in the Dalai Lama's absence. My second-favorite monk was standing in the center of the room overseeing one workman who was up a ladder, unhooking the curtains, while another was perched on a stool giving the light fixture a good wipe.

My relationship with Chogyal went through a subtle change every time His Holiness traveled. In the mornings, when he arrived at work, he would come through to the Dalai Lama's quarters just to see me, spending a few minutes brushing my coat with my special comb and talking to me about that day's events, a reassurance I appreciated after spending the night alone.

Similarly, before he left work at night, he would ensure that my biscuit bowl was filled and my water replenished, then take time to stroke me and remind me how much I was loved, not only by His Holiness but by everyone in the household. I knew that Chogyal was trying to make up for the Dalai Lama's absence, and his kind heart endeared him to me all the more.

But this morning I was alarmed by what he was doing to our bedroom. One of his underlings was gathering items for washing when Chogyal gestured to my beige fleece blanket, on the floor under a chair. "That one," he said. "It hasn't been washed for months."

No, it hadn't—deliberately! Nor would it be, if His Holiness had anything to do with it.

I meowed plaintively.

Chogyal turned to see me sitting in the door with a pleading expression in my eyes. However, for all his warmth of heart, Chogyal was not very perceptive when it came to cats. Unlike the Dalai Lama, who would have known exactly why I was unhappy, he mistook my meow as one of general distress.

Reaching down, he drew me into his arms and began to stroke me.

"Don't worry, HHC," he said reassuringly, using my official designation, short for His Holiness's Cat, at the exact moment that the cleaner seized the blanket and made off with it in the direction of the laundry. "Everything will be back, perfectly clean, before you know it."

Didn't he realize that was exactly the problem? I struggled from his arms, even extending my claws to show I meant business. After a few moments of unpleasantness, he put me down.

"Cats," he said, shaking his head with a bemused smile, as though I had spurned his affections for no good reason.

Returning to the windowsill, my tail hanging dejectedly, I noticed how unpleasantly bright the day had become. Outside, the birds squawked loudly, and the stink of pine was as strong as bathroom disinfectant. How could Chogyal not see what he was doing? How could he not realize that he had just ordered the obliteration of the last surviving link I had to the very cutest kitten that ever lived, my darling little Snow Cub?

Four months earlier, as a result of a dalliance with a ruggedly handsome if ultimately unsuitable back-alley Tom, I had given birth to a gorgeous litter of four. The first three to emerge into the world were just like their father: dark, robust, and male. It was, in fact, a source of general amazement that such vigorous specimens of tabby, soon sporting mackerel stripes, could have emerged from my petite and refined, if delightfully fluffy body. The fourth and final kitten was, however, in every way her mother's child. The last to make her way onto the yak blanket on His Holiness's bed in the early hours one morning, she was born so small she could easily have fit into a tablespoon. Initially we all feared for her survival, and to this day I'm convinced it was only thanks to the Dalai Lama that she made it.

Tibetan Buddhists regard His Holiness as an emanation of Chenrezig, the Buddha of Compassion. While I live in the presence of his compassion all the time, I never felt it directed so powerfully as in our hour of greatest need. As my little baby—a tiny, pink, wrinkled speck with a few wisps of whiteness—struggled for her life, His Holiness watched over us, reciting a mantra softly under his breath. With the spotlight of his attention focused on us until the little one recovered from the birth process, it was as though no bad could come to us. We were bathed in the love and well-being of all the Buddhas. When finally she found her way to a teat and began to suckle, it was as though we had passed through a storm. Thanks to His Holiness's protection, all would be well.

For several weeks before the kittens were born, as news of my pregnancy had spread, His Holiness's office had received entreaties to adopt my kittens from monks across the courtyard at Namgyal Monastery, from friends and supporters elsewhere in India and the Himalayas, and from as far afield as Madrid, Los Angeles, even Sydney. Had I been able to deliver enough of them, my progeny could have been living on every continent of the world.

For the first few weeks my babies were fragile and dependent. After a month, my three boisterous sons were ready to try out canned kitten food, although I still had to nurse my little girl, who was so much tinier than the others. By eight weeks, the boys were running wild—scampering up curtains, tearing through His Holiness's apartment, springing to attack the ankles of unsuspecting passersby.

Before any VIP visitor arrived, the apartment would have to be swept for kittens. Chogyal, who although highly intelligent was not the most coordinated of humans, would fumble about on his hands and knees, tripping over his own robes, as he chased after one or another of my elusive sons. Tenzin—older, taller, and worldly wise—would remove his jacket with some ceremony before adopting a strategic approach, creating a distraction to flush the kittens out of wherever they were hiding and then seizing them when they least expected.

The turning point came with the arrival of one particular visitor. As His Holiness's Cat I have learned to be the very model of discretion when it comes to celebrity visits. Far be it from me to utter the name of any such VIP. Let me just say that this particular guest was a household name, a movie star, an Austrian-born bodybuilder who not only became one of the hottest tickets in Hollywood but went on to be governor of California.

There. That's as far as I'm prepared to go. I couldn't possibly say more without giving the game away.

The afternoon that he arrived in the back of a shiny SUV, Chogyal and Tenzin had undertaken their now-routine kitten check, securing the three tabby kittens in the staff room. Or so they thought.

Picture, if you will, the following scene. The distinguished guest arrived—handsome, charismatic, and towering over the Dalai Lama. As is Tibetan tradition in meeting a high lama, the guest bowed and presented His Holiness with a white scarf, called a *kata,* that His Holiness in turn draped around the VIP's neck. Everything was smiles and serenity—the usual case when the Dalai

Lama is involved. Then the VIP guest stepped beside his host for the official photograph.

A fraction of a second before the photographer snapped the picture, my three sons launched what can only be described as a full frontal assault. Two of them burst out from behind an armchair and charged directly up the visitor's legs. The third sank his claws and teeth into the visitor's left ankle.

The visitor doubled over with shock and pain. The photographer let out a screech of alarm. For a few stunned moments time seemed to stop. Then the first two kittens scampered back down the VIP's legs while the third darted away without so much as an *"Hasta la vista,* baby."

His Holiness, the only one who seemed unsurprised by the feline security lapse, apologized profusely. Recovering his poise, the VIP guest seemed to find the whole thing quite amusing.

I don't think I will ever forget the sight of what happened next: the Dalai Lama was gesturing in the direction of the miscreant kittens, while one of the world's most famous action heroes lay on his stomach, trying to scoop the little wretches from their hiding place under a sofa.

Yes, it was agreed by everyone a short while later, more suitable homes had to be found for the male kittens. But the little one, delicate and docile, a miniature version of her Himalayan mother? In their hearts I don't think anyone wanted to think about her leaving. For the moment, she was safe.

Like many felines, I am a cat of many names. At the Himalaya Book Café, I had been named Rinpoche. In official circles at Jokhang, where His Holiness the Dalai Lama is referred to as HHDL, I acquired the formal title HHC for His Holiness's Cat. My little girl was soon to follow, being given the official appellation HHK—His Holiness's Kitten. But the name that mattered most to me was the one given to her by His Holiness himself. A day or two after the boys were gone he lifted my baby up in his hand and gazed into her eyes with that look of pure love that makes your whole being glow.

"So beautiful, just like your mother!" he murmured, stroking her tiny face with his forefinger. "Aren't you, little Snow Cub?"

For the next few weeks it was just the three of us: His Holiness; me, his Snow Lion; and my daughter, Snow Cub. When I got up early in the morning to curl up next to His Holiness as he meditated, little Snow Cub got up as well, nestling in the warmth of my body. When I went through to the executive assistants' office, she came with me, mewing until she was picked up and placed on their desks, where she loved nothing more than pawing their pens to the edge, then gleefully flicking them to the ground. On one occasion, Tenzin, who sat opposite Chogyal and was a firm advocate of green tea, left his desk and on it, his glass of tea. He returned to find HHK tentatively lapping from the glass. She didn't stop as he got closer, or even when he sat in his chair, put his elbows on his desk, and observed her closely.

"I don't suppose there's any chance of my having some of that, is there, HHK?" he asked dryly.

HHK looked up with an expression of wide-eyed wonderment. Was not everything at Jokhang there specifically for her amusement?

Then came the day that Lobsang, His Holiness's translator, reminded the Dalai Lama of a commitment he had once made. "The queen of Bhutan has asked me to pass on her warm regards, Your Holiness," he told the

Dalai Lama one afternoon after they'd finished working on a transcript.

His Holiness smiled. "Very good. I enjoyed her visit very much. Please send her my very best wishes."

Lobsang nodded. "She also asked after HHC."

"Oh, yes. I remember little Snow Lion sitting on her lap. Quite unusual." He turned to look at where I was curled up with Snow Cub on the beige fleece blanket he had put on the sill after the arrival of the kittens.

"You may remember, Your Holiness, her request to adopt a kitten if HHC ever had any," Lobsang ventured.

The Dalai Lama paused for a moment before meeting Lobsang's eyes. "That's right. I think she was hoping for a kitten with the right . . . how do you call it?"

"Pedigree?" suggested Lobsang.

His Holiness nodded. "We were never able to trace where HHC came from. The family in Delhi who owned her mother had moved away. As for the father of her kittens . . ." The two men exchanged a smile.

"But," continued His Holiness very softly, following Lobsang's gaze to the tiny form beside me, "little Snow Cub does look very much like her mother. And a promise is a promise."

Snow Cub was gone within a week. Lobsang, traveling back to Bhutan on leave, took her himself. For me, the satisfaction of knowing she had gone to one of the best homes imaginable was far outweighed by the sadness of her departure, the reality of once again being alone on the sill.

With his typical compassion, His Holiness moved the beige blanket to the floor underneath a chair in our bedroom so that I wouldn't be constantly reminded of my loss every time I jumped onto the windowsill. But I could still curl up in it under the chair and inhale the smell of little Snow Cub and her brothers, and see wisps of their fur—tiny strands of white interlaced with brown. Some mornings instead of sitting beside His Holiness to meditate, I'd walk over to the fleece blanket and settle there instead, absorbed in my own reveries of the past. And there were other times of day when, with nothing more interesting to absorb me, I would return to the blanket and my memories, bittersweet as they were.

Now, with the spring cleaning in full gear, even the blanket had been taken from me.

Only a day or two after Chogyal's spring cleaning of our apartment, I decided to follow Serena when she left the Himalaya Book Café. She repeated the same pattern every day. At 5:30 P.M., she would disappear into the manager's office, a small room next to the kitchen, reemerging about ten minutes later in her yoga clothes—black, free-trade, organic cotton—with her hair pulled back in a ponytail. Instead of leaving by the front door of the restaurant, she would slip through the kitchen and out the back door, making her way along the lane behind the restaurant and up the winding street I knew all too well.

From time to time Serena spoke about going to yoga in a reverential tone that revealed its great importance to her; her attendance each evening was nonnegotiable. Since arriving back in India she had set out to achieve greater balance in her life and in so doing had embarked on a journey of self-discovery that included not just Indian banquets but much bigger questions about what she wanted to do with her life and where she wanted to do it. Because I possessed the usual feline curiosity, not to mention plenty of free time in the evenings now that His Holiness was away, I wondered what it was about yoga that had such a powerful effect. Wasn't *yoga* simply a name given by humans to the variety of bodily contortions they attempted in a manner vastly inferior to what was achieved quite effortlessly by us cats?

Keeping up with Serena as she approached the summit of the hill wasn't easy for a cat with wonky pins. But what I lacked in physical strength, I made up for in determination. A short while after she approached a modest-looking bungalow with faded Tibetan prayer flags looped under the eaves, I followed her inside.

The front door was ajar, leading into a small hallway where there was a large shoe rack, mostly empty, and a heady perfume of shoe leather, perspiration, and Nag Champa incense.

A beaded curtain separated the hall from the yoga studio. Above it was a sign that spelled out the name, The Downward Dog School of Yoga, in faded letters. Pushing my way through the strings of beads, I found myself in a very large room. At the far end a man was standing in what I later learned was *Virabhadrasana II,* Warrior II Pose. With his arms stretched wide at shoulder height, he cut a majestic figure, silhouetted against a panoramic vista of the Himalayas, visible through the open floor-to-ceiling doors. The icy summits reflected the setting sun, which crowned the peaks in gold.

"We seem to have a visitor," said the man in warrior pose, in a mellow voice with a faint German accent. His white hair was cropped close to his head, but despite his apparent age, there was a suppleness about him. His face was tanned and timeless, his eyes a vibrant blue. I wondered how he knew I was in the room, until I saw that one whole wall of the studio was mirrored, and I realized he had seen me coming through the beaded curtain.

Out on the balcony, Serena turned and saw me. "Oh, Rinpoche, you followed me!" Walking toward me, she told the man in Warrior Pose, "This little one spends a lot of time at the café. I don't suppose you let cats inside the studio, do you?"

There was a pause before he answered. "Not as a rule. But I have a sense that your friend is rather special."

I had no idea exactly why he sensed this, but I was happy to take it as permission to stay. Without further ado, I hopped onto a low wooden stool near a rack of blankets at the back of the room. It was the perfect place from which to observe without being observed.

Looking around, I noticed a small, framed black-and-white photograph of a dog hanging on the wall. It was a Lhasa Apso, the same breed as Kyi Kyi. Popular among Tibetans, Lhasa Apsos traditionally served as monastery sentinels, alerting monks to the presence of intruders. Was this particular Lhasa Apso the dog after which the Downward Dog School of Yoga was named?

Other people began arriving for class. Mostly expatriates, with a sprinkling of Indians, the mix of men and women seemed to range in age from the 30s on up. They carried themselves with a certain awareness, an indefinable poise. Spreading out yoga mats, bolsters, and blankets, they lay on their backs with their eyes shut and their legs strapped together as though impersonating the rows of trussed chickens I used to see in the market.

After a while, the instructor, whom people were calling *Ludo,* stood at the front and addressed the 20 or so students, his voice gentle but clear. "Yoga is *vidya,*" he said, "which is Sanskrit for being with life as it is, not life as I would like it to be. Not life *if only* this was different, or *if only* I could do that.

"So, how do we begin yoga? By getting out of our heads and into the present moment. The only moment that actually exists is the here and now."

Through the open studio doors came the shrill cries of swifts, soaring and swooping in the late afternoon. Stray chords of Hindi music and the clatter of cooking pots rose from the houses down the hill, along with the aromas of evening meals being prepared.

"Abiding in the here and now," Ludo continued, "we recognize that in each unfolding moment, everything is complete. Everything is interconnected. But we cannot experience this directly until we let go of thought and simply relax, until we acknowledge that we have come to this moment, here and now, only because everything else is the way it is.

"Relax in open awareness," Ludo told the students. "The unification of life. This is yoga."

Ludo then led the class through a sequence of *asanas,* or postures, some standing, some seated, some dynamic, some resting.

Yoga, I realized, was not just about developing flexibility of the body. It went beyond that.

Along with his instructions on how to bend and stretch, Ludo gave out gems of wisdom that pointed to a much broader purpose. "We cannot work on the body unless we also work on the mind. When we come across constrictions—obstacles in our physical practice—we discover that physiology is a mirror of psychology. Mind and body can get stuck in grooves that cause discomfort, stress, and tightness."

When one of the men mentioned that he couldn't bend over and place his palms on the floor because his hamstrings were too tight, Ludo remarked, "Hamstrings, yes. For some that is the challenge. For others it is being able to turn. Or simply to sit cross-legged comfortably. The dissatisfactions of life manifest in many different forms. Exactly how they are expressed is unique to each one of us. But yoga provides us with the space to become free." As he walked along the rows of students, making subtle adjustments to their postures, he continued. "Instead of going round and round, deepening the same subconscious habits of body and mind, use your awareness. Don't try to avoid tightness by getting into a compromised posture; instead breathe through it! Not with force but with wisdom. Use your breath to create openness. Breath by breath, subtle change is possible. Each breath is a step to transformation."

I followed the class with keen interest from my stool at the back, pleased to have remained unobserved. But when Ludo instructed the students to perform a seated twist, suddenly 20 heads turned and faced me. Instantly there were smiles and a few chuckles.

"Ah, yes—today's special guest," said Ludo.

"All that white hair!" someone exclaimed.

"Blue eyes," said another.

Then, as all 20 pairs of eyes were trained on me, a man remarked, "Must be Swami."

This provoked laughter as people were reminded of the local sage whose image appeared on posters all over town.

I was relieved when the twist ended but immediately found myself being observed once again, when everyone turned toward me in the opposite direction.

At the end of the class, as they lay on their mats in *Shavasana,* the pose of the corpse, Ludo told the students, "In some ways this is the most challenging pose of all. Calm body and calm mind. Try not to engage with every thought. Simply acknowledge the thought, accept it, and let it go. We can discover far more in the space between thoughts than when we become absorbed in conceptual elaboration. In the stillness we discover that there are other ways of knowing things than through the intellect."

After class, as the students were putting away their blankets and blocks and bolsters, a few paused to speak to me. While some returned to the hallway to put on their shoes and leave, most congregated on the balcony beyond the sliding doors. An assortment of chairs with brightly colored cushions and a few beanbag chairs were ranged along a faded Indian carpet that ran the length of the balcony. At a table stacked with mugs and glasses, someone was pouring water and green tea as the students settled into what was evidently a comfortable postclass routine.

We cats are not fond of too much noise or movement, so I waited until they were all seated before slipping silently from the stool and making my way out to the balcony next to Serena. The final rays of the setting sun had turned the mountains a gleaming coral red.

"Trying to breathe through discomfort when we're

doing yoga is one thing," a gravel-voiced woman called Merrilee was saying. She had joined the class almost at the end, as though she had really come only for the social part of the evening. And was it my imagination, or had she surreptitiously slipped something from a hip flask into her glass? "But what about when we're not doing yoga and we have to deal with problems?" she asked.

"All is yoga,'" Ludo told her. "Usually we react to challenges in a habitual way, with anger or avoidance. By breathing through a challenge, we can arrive at a more useful response."

"Isn't anger or avoidance sometimes a useful reaction?" asked Ewing, an older American who was a longtime resident of McLeod Ganj. Occasionally he visited the Himalaya Book Café, where it was said that he had fled to India after some sort of tragedy back home. For many years he had played piano in the lobby of New Delhi's Grand Hotel.

"A *reaction* is automatic, habitual," Ludo said. "A *response* is considered. That's the difference. What's important is to create space, to open ourselves up to possibilities beyond the habitual, which rarely serve us well. Anger is never an enlightened response. We may be wrathful—speaking in mock-angry tones to stop a child who is about to step near a fire, for example—but that's very different from real anger."

"The problem," observed a tall Indian man sitting next to Serena, "is that we get stuck in our comfort zone, even when it isn't very comfortable."

"Clinging to the familiar," Serena agreed. "To things that used to give us such happiness but don't anymore."

I looked up at her, startled, when she said this. I was thinking of the beige fleece blanket in the bedroom and how memories of the many happy times I had spent on it with my little Snow Cub were now laced with sadness.

"Shantideva, the Indian Buddhist sage, talks about licking honey off the edge of a blade," said Ludo. "No matter how sweet, the price we pay is much higher."

"So how do we know," asked Serena, "when something that has been positive in the past has outlived its usefulness?"

Ludo looked over at her with eyes so clear they seemed almost silver. "When it causes us to suffer," he replied simply. *"Suffer* comes from a Latin word meaning *to carry.* And while pain is sometimes unavoidable, suffering is not. For instance, we may have a very happy relationship with someone, and then we lose the person. We feel pain, of course: that's natural. But when we continue to carry that pain, feeling constantly bereft, that's suffering."

There was a pause while everyone absorbed this. In the deepening twilight, the mountains loomed in the distance, brooding shadows skimmed with vivid pink like the frosting on Mrs. Trinci's cupcakes.

"I sometimes think the past is a dangerous place to go looking for happiness," said the Indian man sitting next to Serena.

"You're right, Sid," agreed Ludo. "The only time we can experience happiness is in this moment, here and now."

Later, the students began to drift away. Serena left with several others, and I followed her into the hall.

"I see little Swami is with you," observed one of the women, slipping on her shoes.

"Yes. We know each other well. She spends a lot of

time at the café. I'm giving her a lift back there now,"
Serena said, picking me up.

"What's her real name?" another woman asked.

"Oh, she's a cat of many names. Everywhere she goes
she seems to acquire another one."

"Then today is no exception," said Sid. Taking a yellow daisy from a vase in the hallway, he fashioned it into
a flower garland and placed it around my neck. "I prostrate to you, little Swami," he said, bringing his smooth,
manicured hands together at his heart. As I looked into
his eyes, I saw great tenderness.

Then he was opening the door for Serena, and we
were making our way back down the hill.

"We are so lucky to have such a wonderful teacher,"
said Serena.

"Yes," agreed Sid. "Ludvig—Ludo—is exceptional."

"My mother says he's been in McLeod Ganj as long
as I've been alive."

Sid nodded. "Since the early '60s. He came at the
request of Heinrich Harrer."

"Of *Seven Years in Tibet* fame?" asked Serena. "The
Dalai Lama's tutor?"

"That's right. Heinrich arranged an introduction to
the Dalai Lama very soon after Ludo came to McLeod
Ganj. It is said that he and His Holiness are good friends.
In fact, it was His Holiness who encouraged Ludo to set
up the yoga studio."

"I didn't know that," Serena said. Glancing at Sid, she
was suddenly aware of how much he knew of local affairs.
After a few moments, she decided to test this further.
"There's a guy walking behind us in a dark jacket, felt
cap," she said under her breath. "Someone said he's the
Maharajah of Himachal Pradesh. Is that true?"

They continued down the hill for a while before Sid discreetly glanced over his shoulder. "I've heard the same thing," he said.

"I've seen him around here quite often," Serena said.

"So have I," observed Sid. "Perhaps he usually takes a walk at this time of day?"

"Could be," mused Serena.

The very next day I was padding along the corridor of the executive wing when Lobsang called out to me. "HHC! Come here, my little one! There's something you'll want to see."

I ignored him, of course. We cats are not given to kowtowing to every plea, entreaty, or even humble petition made by humans. What good would it do? You are so much more grateful when we do eventually throw you a bone—if you'll excuse the whiff of dog about that particular metaphor.

Lobsang was not to be deterred, however, and moments later I was being picked up, taken to his office, and placed on his desk.

"I'm Skyping Bhutan," he told me. "And I spotted someone I thought you'd like to see."

His computer screen revealed a sumptuously furnished room and to one side of it, a window seat on which a Himalayan cat was lying on her back, sunning her tummy. She had her head tilted back, her eyes closed, and her legs and bushy tail splayed in what Ludo might have termed "the pose of the starfish." For cats, this is the most defenseless, trusting, and contented of all poses.

It took me a few moments before I realized . . . Could it really be? Yes, it was! But how she had grown!

"Her official title is HRHC," Lobsang told me. "Her Royal Highness's Cat. So one more letter than HHC. And they tell me she is as adored at the palace there as you are here at Namgyal."

I watched the rise and fall of Snow Cub's tummy as she dozed in the sun, remembering how miserable I'd been just days earlier when Chogyal had removed the beige blanket from the bedroom and with it had deprived me of the tender memories of my little girl.

Or so I'd felt at the time.

Since then I had come to learn that my unhappiness had been inflicted not by Chogyal but, unintentionally, by myself. By wallowing in my own nostalgic memories, spending so much time thinking about a relationship that had moved on, I had been needlessly carrying pain. Suffering.

Meanwhile, Snow Cub had grown into a new life as the beloved palace cat of the queen of Bhutan. Could any mother wish for more?

Turning, I stepped closer to where Lobsang was sitting at his desk and bent down to massage his fingers with my face.

"HHC!" he exclaimed. "You've never done that before!"

As he responded by scratching my neck, I closed my eyes and began to purr. Ludo was right: happiness was not to be found in the past. Not in trying to relive memories, however beguiling.

It could only be experienced in this moment, here and now.

CHAPTER THREE

What would happen, dear reader, if you were to achieve your most longed-for dream? What if you were to succeed in your chosen ambition, beyond your wildest hopes?

There's no harm in contemplating this happy prospect, is there? Imagine, for example, opening the front door of a beautiful home and discovering your family inside, a picture-book image of familial bliss and pleasing demeanors, with delightful aromas wafting from the kitchen and no squabbling over the TV remote.

Or, in my own case, venturing into the cold storage room of the kitchen downstairs to discover 10,000 portions of Mrs. Trinci's diced chicken liver, stowed in pristine condition and awaiting my personal delectation.

What an enchanting prospect! How alluring the image!

Little did we know down at the Himalaya Book Café that someone who had achieved something equally amazing was about to enter our midst.

We barely noticed him at first. As it happened, his initial arrival coincided with one of my own late-morning appearances. It was shortly after 11 when I made my way down the road from Jokhang at the exact moment he happened to be striding toward the café. He was a rugged-looking, middle-aged man with auburn hair graying at the temples, a craggy face, beetle brows, and inquisitive eyes. There was a marked contrast between his face, lined and lived-in, and his expensive outfit—cream linen jacket, cream pants, gleaming gold watch. He was walking faster than the meandering stroll of most tourists and carrying several guidebooks on the travel highlights of northwest India.

I made my way through the café, pausing to touch noses with Marcel and Kyi Kyi in their basket under the counter. With Franc's departure and the arrival of Serena and Sam, it was as though an invisible thread had drawn us nonhuman denizens of the café closer. Having been through all the changes together gave us a shared experience, a common bond. Not that it went any further than a touch on the nose and polite inquiry. You wouldn't expect me to climb into their basket with them, would you? I'm not that kind of cat, and, dear reader, this is certainly not that kind of book!

Taking up my usual position on the magazine rack, I observed our nattily dressed visitor as he made himself comfortable on one of the nearby banquettes. Summoning a waiter with an imperious hand, when he spoke it was with a Scottish burr: "Has lunch service started?"

Sanjay, a fresh-faced young waiter in a crisp, white uniform, nodded.

"I'll have a glass of your Sémillon Sauvignon Blanc," the visitor told him. Spreading his travel books across the table in front of him and taking a cell phone from his pocket, he soon appeared to be busy researching travel plans, cross-checking details from one book to another, and keying them into his phone.

When the glass of Sémillon Sauvignon Blanc arrived, he took a tentative first sip, swirling the liquid around in his mouth with a searching expression. Thereafter he didn't so much drink the wine as inhale it. Four sips and, only a few minutes later, his glass was empty.

This fact didn't escape the attention of Headwaiter Kusali, whose omniscience was legendary. He dispatched Sanjay with the bottle of SSB to freshen the visitor's glass. A third glass, then a fourth soon followed before the visitor asked for his bill, cleared away his books, and left.

It was half an hour later when developments took an unusual turn. Looking up from my own lunchtime treat— a delicious serving of smoked salmon cut into dainty, bite-size strips—who should I see at the café entrance but the same man, this time accompanied by his wife.

A matronly woman with a kind face and sensible shoes, she glanced around the café with an expression of appreciation. It was one we were quite used to. By the time many Westerners had made their way up to McLeod Ganj from Delhi, they were overwhelmed by India, with its chaos, crowds, poverty, traffic, and shocking vibrancy. The moment they stepped through the doors of the Himalaya Book Café, however, they found themselves in altogether different aesthetics. To the right of an ornate reception counter, the café had a soft-lit, classic quality, with its white tablecloths, cane chairs, and a large, brass espresso machine. Richly embroidered Tibetan Buddhist wall hangings, or *thangkas*, bedecked the walls. To the left-hand side of the counter and up a few steps was the bookstore section, its well-stocked shelves interspersed with a treasure trove of lavish cards, Himalayan artifacts, and other gifts. It was an exotic fusion of casual European chic and Buddhist mysticism.

Many visitors, on first encountering this, heave a visible sigh of relief.

The visitor's wife wasn't quite so emphatic. As she looked anxiously at her husband, she seemed to be hoping the café would suit him, which it did. Eminently!

Stepping forward to greet them, Kusali showed them to a window table, where the husband studied both menu and wine list as if for the first time, before ordering precisely the same bottle of wine. On this occasion he sipped his SSB with slightly more restraint, but during the course of the lunch, he sailed effortlessly through most of the bottle with minimal help from his wife.

Watching the two of them from a distance, I sensed something awkward about the way they were together. There were long pauses in their conversation, during which they looked everywhere but at each other, followed by exchanges that soon petered out.

Most Western visitors had such busy itineraries that they would visit the café only once or twice during the course of a brief stay. Not our dapper friend and his wife. The very next morning at 11 A.M., the hallowed moment at which alcohol was served, he arrived at the café, walked to the banquette, and ordered a glass of SSB. Foreseeing a rerun of the previous day's events, Kusali made a gracious appearance, pouring the visitor's wine personally before suggesting, "Would you like me to bring a wine bucket to your table, sir?"

The visitor decided that, on balance, yes, he would. Helping himself to refills as he paged through a travel brochure with somewhat less interest than the day before, he soon dispatched the contents of the bottle.

Once again, half an hour after leaving, he reappeared at the café entrance with his wife, this time telling Kusali, who was at the reception desk, that they had enjoyed the previous day's visit so much they had decided to return. The ever-diplomatic Kusali smiled politely as this official, somewhat edited version of events was established.

Dear reader, would you believe me if I told you that the exact same *Groundhog Day* reenactment occurred the following morning? Well, perhaps not exactly. On day three, the visitor walked straight through the door to "his" banquette at 11 o'clock, whereupon Kusali had a waiter deliver his preferred wine in an ice bucket. Serena, who had been on a visit to Delhi for the two previous days to order new kitchen equipment, watched this happen and approached Kusali a short while later, eyebrows raised. During their tête-à-tête, when the visitor stared at his cell phone with a somewhat downcast expression, Kusali indicated it was safe for her to look in that direction.

As soon as she did, she froze. Then she quickly ended her conversation with Kusali and headed toward the bookstore. Moments later she was standing beside Sam, who was sitting behind the counter at his computer.

"Can I jump on for a minute?" she asked urgently.

"Sure." As he slid off his stool she quickly opened a search engine.

Gordon Finlay. Sam read the name as she keyed it into the search field.

"You know who he is?" she whispered.

He shook his head.

"I think he's over there," she said, tipping her head in the direction of the banquette. "Bagpipe Burgers."

Sam's face lit up. "That's him?"

The two of them stared at the Wikipedia entry, which featured a photograph of the Bagpipe Burgers founder.

"'Started as a single-outlet burger bar in Inverness, Scotland,'" Sam was reading. "'Now one of the biggest fast-food franchises in the world.'" Skimming down the page, he pulled out highlights: "valued at half a billion dollars"; "presence in every major market"; "famous tartan uniforms"; "creators of the gourmet burger"; "commitment to quality."

"Is it him?" Serena prompted.

Sam studied the photograph in front of them before turning to look at the restaurant patron. "Our guy looks . . . less jowly."

Serena snipped her index and middle fingers together. "Dr. Knife."

"You know about the drinking these past couple of days?" Sam asked her.

"Occupational hazard in our line of work."

Sam gazed intently into her eyes. "But what's he doing in McLeod Ganj?"

"That's what I'm . . ." She reached over him to the keyboard and tapped in something else, nodding as another page opened up on the screen. "Yup. This happened when I was leaving London. He cashed out for five hundred million dollars."

"That guy over there?" whispered Sam, wide-eyed.

"Exactly." Serena squeezed his arm before stepping away from the counter for another discreet peek.

She nodded. "People in London couldn't stop talking about it. It's every entrepreneur's dream, and for the restaurant business, it's an inconceivable amount of money. People either love him or hate him."

"Which side are you on?"

"Admire him, of course! What he did is amazing. He got into a sector with a whole lot of poor-quality associations and created something that was genuinely distinctive. People liked it, and it took off. He made a pile of money, but it took him twenty years of incredibly hard work."

"Weird guy, though," Sam said, shaking his head.

"You mean the multiple visits?"

"Not only that. You know, he spends hours in the Internet Shop down the road."

It was Serena's turn to look surprised.

The Internet Shop, which catered to an almost entirely local clientele, was dirty, overcrowded, and poorly lit.

"I see him going in there every morning." Sam lived in an apartment over the café with windows facing the street. "He's there from eight in the morning. Afterward, he comes here."

Over the next week, Gordon Finlay was a regular fixture at the Himalaya Book Café. He did miss a couple of mornings, during which the rear banquette felt curiously vacant. On the first occasion he and his wife were seen climbing into the back of a tour van that took visitors on all-day excursions through the surrounding countryside. On the other occasion, a waiter reported having seen him in conversation with Amrit, one of the vendors who plied their trade beneath the tangled chaos of telephone wires along the street.

Of all the vendors, the ragged Amrit was the youngest and least popular, struggling to interest passers in the deep-fried dumplings he retrieved from a filthy-looking pan. What Gordon Finlay found of interest about the ever-disconsolate Amrit was hard to fathom. But when Finlay missed both his preprandial bottle of wine and his lunch, Kusali looked out the window and noticed that Amrit was no longer at his stall.

The mystery was solved the next day when Amrit was seen back in position, in bright yellow-and-red overalls and cap, with the blackened pan replaced by a shiny silver outdoor-barbecue wok and jaunty bunting fluttering around a *Happy Chicken* sign. As he flipped chicken breasts for a growing line of customers, Gordon Finlay stood behind him in his trademark cream jacket, giving instructions.

At 11 o'clock sharp, Finlay was back in the café.

Exactly what Gordon Finlay was doing in McLeod Ganj became a subject of growing conjecture. Surely he hadn't picked this modest little town in the Himalaya foothills as the starting point for a new global fast-food chain? Why bother coming here only to spend so much time drinking? Wouldn't somewhere in Italy or the South of France be more agreeable for this? And what about all the time he spent in the Internet Shop, when he could so easily have gone online from the far greater comfort of his hotel?

I am pleased, dear reader, to claim a vital part in discovering the answer to these and other open questions. Like many of life's most intriguing developments, this one didn't arise from any deliberate action on my part. My simple, if admittedly irresistible, presence was all that was required to unleash the most unexpected flow of pent-up emotion.

Occupying my usual spot in the café, I had adopted what Ludo might have called *the pose of Mae West,* lying on my side with my head propped up on my right front paw. It was getting close to the time that Gordon Finlay usually made the first of his two daily appearances. But when I glanced up from where I had begun to groom the fluffy white fur on my tummy, who should appear at the door but Mrs. Finlay. She looked anxiously about the restaurant before making her way toward the book shop. She had never ventured this far before; she and her husband usually occupied the same table closer to the front. She had almost reached the magazine rack before Serena approached her.

"I'm looking for my husband," Mrs. Finlay told Serena. "We've been here a few times."

Serena nodded with a smile.

"It's become his favorite place in Dharamsala, and I was hoping . . ." Her lower lip was quivering, and she drew a deep breath to compose herself. "I was hoping I might find him here."

"We haven't seen him today," said Serena. "But you're very welcome to wait." She was gesturing toward the banquette at the back, the one at which Gordon Finlay enjoyed his morning bottle of wine, when for the first time Mrs. Finlay looked at the shelf where I was grooming myself.

Sensing I was being stared at, I looked directly at her.

"Oh, good heavens!" Mrs. Finlay's already fragile composure was threatened again. "Just like our little Sapphire."

Stepping toward me, she reached out to stroke my neck. I looked into her red-rimmed eyes and purred.

"This is Rinpoche," Serena told her, but Mrs. Finlay wasn't listening. First one tear, then another began to roll down her cheek. Biting her lip to stem the flow, she stopped petting me and reached into her handbag for a tissue. But it was too much. Within moments she had let out a great sob of emotion. Serena put her arm around her and gently guided her to the banquette.

For a while Mrs. Finlay wept quietly into her tissue. Serena gestured toward Kusali for a glass of water.

"I'm sorry," she apologized after a while. "I'm so . . ."

Serena shushed her.

"We had a little one, just like her," Mrs. Finlay said, gesturing toward me. "It took me back. All those years ago in Scotland, Sapphire was so special to us. She used to sleep on our bed every night." She gulped. "Things were different then."

A waiter arrived with a glass of water. Mrs. Finlay took a sip.

"They *are* very special," agreed Serena, glancing at me.

But Mrs. Finlay wasn't listening as she stared at the table while putting down the glass. She seemed transfixed. Until, that is, she somehow felt moved to confess, "Gordon—that's my husband—is *hating* being here." She said it as though unburdening herself of a terrible admission.

Serena allowed a moment to pass before telling her, "That's not an unusual reaction, you know. For Western visitors coming here, not sure what to expect, India can be a real shock."

Mrs. Finlay shook her head. "No, it's not that. We both know India well." For the first time she met Serena's gaze. "Gordon has been here many times over the years. That's why he chose it as the place to spend our first month of retirement. Only . . . it isn't working."

She seemed to be drawing strength from Serena's compassionate presence, her voice less broken as she continued. "He's just had a big success, you see, selling a business after twenty-odd years building it up. Gordon's a very hard-working man. Determined. You can't begin to imagine the sacrifices he's made. Years and years of eighteen-hour workdays. Missing out on vacations. Always having to leave birthday parties and dinners and family celebrations early. 'It will all be worth it'—that's what he's always said. 'I'll retire early, and we'll have the time of our lives.' He always believed it. I did, too. It didn't matter how much we had to give up. We'd be happy when . . ." She looked pensive for a while, then began again. "It was all right for the first couple of weeks. He was a changed man, free to do as he liked. But it didn't last. Suddenly there were no calls or messages or meetings. No decisions to make. No one wanting to know what he thought. It was as if an elastic band that had been stretched to the limit suddenly let go.

"When he was working so frenetically," she went on, "the idea of all the time in the world seemed like heaven. Instead, he's finding it a terrible burden. He didn't bring his laptop with him. It was a part of his old life. But when he goes out in the mornings—he says for a walk—I'm sure he's going to one of those Internet places." Mrs. Finlay was looking at Serena, whose even expression gave not the slightest inkling that she knew Mrs. Finlay's suspicions were correct.

"And he drinks. He's never been like that before—drinking during the day. I know it's because he's bored and miserable and doesn't know what to do with himself. He said as much this morning before he left the hotel. I've never seen him so unhappy."

As she welled up again, Serena reached out and squeezed her arm. "This, too, will pass," she murmured.

Not trusting herself to speak, Mrs. Finlay nodded.

Mrs. Finlay left the café a short while later, and the couple didn't appear for lunch that day. Only time would tell exactly how she and her husband might resolve their unexpected disappointment; although the subject of the miserable millionaire came up again later that evening at the café.

It was approaching 11 P.M., and the half dozen or so tables of diners remaining were on dessert and coffee. Serena looked up to where Sam was sitting on his stool behind the bookstore counter and caught his eye with a questioning gesture. He responded with a thumbs-up. Only one browser remained in the shop: a pair of ankles and the bottom of a monk's red robe peaked out from beneath one of the bookstore partitions.

Serena headed toward the bookstore for the end-of-the-day ritual. Two heads lifted up from the wicker basket under the counter; Marcel and Kyi Kyi were focusing on the promising direction of Serena's footsteps.

She reached the top of the short flight of steps to the bookstore at the same time the last remaining customer was leaving.

"Lobsang!" She greeted him warmly, stepping forward to embrace him. Lobsang had become a frequent visitor to the bookstore, finding on its shelves a range of Buddhist and recent nonfiction titles that were dazzling compared to what had previously been available in Dharamsala. And thanks to the fact that he and Serena went way back, she had insisted he be given the most generous available discount.

Since their early teen years when they had gotten to know each other while working as Mrs. Trinci's kitchen hands, their lives had taken them on very different trajectories. While Serena had been away in Europe, Lobsang, whose incisive intellect and outstanding language skills had been evident early on, had won a scholarship to Yale to study semiotics. Returning to India to work as the Dalai Lama's translator, he had also evolved in other ways. In particular there was a calming quality about his presence to which other people invariably responded, sometimes visibly leaning back in their chairs and relaxing their shoulders or breaking into a smile.

"Sam and I are about to have a hot chocolate. Would you like to join us?" asked Serena.

For all Lobsang's tranquility, I noticed that something about Serena brought about a change in him. He seemed to find her company a cause of great amusement.

"That would be wonderful," he replied enthusiastically, as he followed her toward the two sofas.

A short while later Kusali arrived with hot chocolate for the humans and a saucer of dog biscuits, which he held over the coffee table for a suspenseful moment, inciting the dogs' desperate anticipation, before placing it down with a Pavlovian *clink* that triggered their frenetic scramble toward the bookstore.

For my own part, I hopped off the shelf and stretched out my back paws, flaring one claw then the other, before crossing the room and nimbly leaping onto the sofa, landing between Serena and Lobsang, who sat facing Sam.

"HHC is very lucky to have you," observed Lobsang, as Serena leaned forward to pour my saucer of milk. "Especially with His Holiness away."

"We feel lucky to have her," said Serena, stroking me. "Don't we, Rinpoche?"

She hadn't yet placed the saucer on the floor, so I stepped onto the coffee table and began lapping up milk.

"Do you allow cats on the table?" Lobsang asked, amused by my audacity.

"Not as a rule," replied Serena, regarding me with an indulgent smile.

For a while all three humans watched in silence as I lapped up the milk with a lusty purr. Was it feline telepathy or just my imagination that Sam wasn't pleased to have Lobsang join their usual end-of-the-day get-together?

Serena asked Lobsang about the project he was currently working on, and he mentioned the commentary on an esoteric text by Pabongka Rinpoche that he was helping translate. Then conversation moved on to what had happened during the day. Serena told them about her encounter with Mrs. Finlay, and how Mr. Finlay's hard-fought vision for early retirement had turned out to be such a bitter disappointment.

Lobsang listened to the story, sympathy pervading his immense calm, before he said, "There are few of us,

I think, who don't make the same mistake. Believing in *I'll be happy when I retire. When I have such and such an amount of money. When I achieve this particular goal.*" He paused, smiling at the absurdity of it. "We create our own superstitions and then persuade ourselves to believe in them."

"Superstitions?" challenged Sam.

Lobsang nodded. "Inventing a relationship between two things that have no connection, like a broken mirror and bad luck, or a black cat and good luck."

Lifting my face from the saucer, I looked over at him at that precise moment. All three of them laughed.

"Or a Himalayan cat," offered Serena, "and *extreme* good luck."

I resumed my lapping.

Lobsang continued. "We begin to believe that our happiness depends on a certain outcome or person or lifestyle. That's the superstition."

"But I have shelves and shelves here"—Sam gestured behind him—"filled with books on goal-setting and positive thinking and manifesting abundance. Are you saying they're all wrong?"

Lobsang chuckled. "Oh, no, that's not what I mean. It can be useful to have goals. Purpose. But we should never believe that our *happiness* depends on achieving them. The two are really quite separate."

There was silence while Sam and Serena digested this, broken only by the sound of my lapping and the dogs' snuffling for crumbs under the table.

"If any object, achievement, or relationship was a true cause of happiness, then whoever had such a thing should be happy. But no such thing has ever been found," continued Lobsang. "What's saddest of all is that if we believe that our happiness depends on something we don't currently have, then we can't be happy here and now. Yet here and now is the only time we *can* be happy. We can't be happy in the future; it doesn't yet exist."

"And when the future arrives," reflected Serena, "we discover that whatever we believed would give us happiness doesn't make us as happy as we thought. Look at Gordon Finlay."

"Exactly," Lobsang said.

Sam was shifting in his seat. "There was a neuroscience study on this not so long ago. I think it was called 'The Disappointment of Success.' It looked at pregoal attainment versus postgoal attainment. Pregoal attainment—the positive feeling people get working toward a goal—is more intense and enduring in terms of brain activity than postgoal attainment, which elicits a short-lived feeling of release."

"Followed by the question, *Is that all there is?*" suggested Serena.

"The journey really is more important than the destination," confirmed Lobsang.

"Which only makes me wonder all the more about going back to Europe," said Serena.

"You might stay?" Lobsang asked, his voice full of hope. When she looked at him, he held her gaze, not just for one or two seconds but until she looked away.

"The night of the Indian banquet was the start of it," Serena explained. "It made me realize how much more fulfilling it is to work for people who really appreciate what I'm doing, instead of for people who go out just to be seen in the right places. Why put myself through all that stress? Look at what happened to Gordon Finlay. He's one of the greatest success stories of the decade in the restaurant world. His success is what tens of thousands of people aspire to. But it made him such a workaholic that he just can't stop. What's the point of having all the success in the world if you have no inner peace?"

Beneath Serena's words I detected other unspoken concerns. Over the past weeks, I'd watched her greeting old school friends who came to visit with their husbands and children. Each time it seemed to me that she was feeling pulled in a very different direction.

The next morning, Gordon Finlay arrived at 10:30 A.M. From the moment he entered the café he looked like a man unburdened. Making his way to his banquette, he ordered an espresso and chose a copy of *The Times of India* from the newsstand.

After flicking through the paper and finishing his coffee, he got up and approached Serena at the counter. "My wife tells me she came in yesterday and you were very kind to her," he began in his Scottish burr. "I just wanted to let you know that I appreciate that. Just as I appreciate your . . . discretion."

"Oh! You're welcome."

"This place has been like an oasis for me," he continued, glancing at the Buddhist *thangkas* hanging on the walls. "We've decided to go home. No idea what I'm going to do, but I can't sit around drinking two bottles of wine a day. My liver wouldn't last long."

"I'm sorry things haven't worked out the way you planned," said Serena. Then almost as an afterthought she added, "I hope there was something about India that you enjoyed?"

Gordon Finlay looked thoughtful for a moment before he nodded. "Funny, the thing that immediately springs to mind is helping that kid down the road get his act together."

Serena laughed. "Happy Chicken?"

"He's doing a roaring business," Finlay said.

"Are you a shareholder?"

"No. But I was only too glad to set him up. He reminded me so much of me when I was starting out: starved for capital, surrounded by competitors, and no product differentiation. All it took was a couple of hundred pounds and a bit of training. Now he's acing it!"

As he spoke, Gordon Finlay seemed to grow taller and stand straighter. For the first time there was a glimpse of the commanding CEO he had been until so recently.

"Perhaps," suggested Serena, "you've just described what you might do next."

"I couldn't rescue every street vendor in the world!" he protested.

"No. But you would change the lives of the ones you did. You obviously got a lot of satisfaction from helping just the one. Imagine the satisfaction from helping many!"

Gordon Finlay stared at her for the longest time, a glint illuminating his dark, observant eyes, before he said, "You know, you just might be on to something."

CHAPTER FOUR

Boredom. It's a terrible affliction, is it not, dear reader? And as far as I can tell, it's an almost universal one. On an everyday level, there's the boredom of being wherever you are and doing whatever task lies ahead, whether you're an executive with a dozen dreary reports to produce before month's end or a cat on a filing cabinet with a whole empty morning to doze through before those deliciously crispy *goujons* of sea trout—perhaps with some clotted cream to follow—are served for lunch down at the café.

How often I overhear tourists say, "I can't wait to get back to civilization"—the very same visitors, I expect, who for several months earlier were eagerly crossing off the days on their calendars in keen anticipation of their once-in-a-lifetime trip to India. "I wish it were Friday" is another variation on the same theme, as if we must somehow endure five days of oppressive tedium for those precious two when we may actually enjoy ourselves.

And the problem goes even deeper. Raising our heads

from this particular batch of month-end reports or this specific empty morning on the filing cabinet, when we think of all those still to come, our boredom slides into a more profound existential despair. *What's the point of it all?* We may find ourselves wondering, *Why bother? Who cares?* Life can seem a bleak and endless exercise in futility.

For those beings with a broader perspective of Planet Earth, boredom is sometimes accompanied by a darker companion—guilt. We know that compared to many others, our lives are actually quite comfortable. We don't live in a war zone or in abject poverty; we don't have to dwell in the shadows on account of our gender or religious opinions. We're free to eat, dress, live, and walk however we like, thank you very much. But even so, we're bored beyond measure.

In my own case, if I can claim mitigating circumstances, the Dalai Lama *had* been away for some days. There was none of the usual bustle of activity and no visits from Mrs. Trinci, lavish with both food and affection. Most of all, there was none of the reassuring energy and love I felt simply by being in His Holiness's presence.

And so, I set out for the café one morning heavy of heart and slow of paw. My customary dawdling was even more dawdling than usual; just moving my rear legs felt like a Herculean effort. *Why was I even doing this?* I asked myself. Delicious though lunch might be, eating it would take me all of five minutes, and then it would be a long wait until dinner.

Little did I realize how events were about to shake me from my lethargy.

It all began with Sam behaving in an unusually urgent manner, leaping off his stool in the bookstore and hurrying down the steps to the café.

"Serena!" He stage-whispered to catch her attention. "It's Franc!" He gestured behind him to his computer screen. Franc was in the habit of Skyping for business updates, but his calls were always on Monday morning at 10 A.M. when the café was quiet, not in the early afternoon when activity was near its peak.

Serena hurried over to the bookstore counter. Sam turned up the speakers and opened a screen revealing Franc in a living room. There were several people behind him sitting on a sofa and in armchairs. His expression was strained.

"My father died last night," Franc announced without preamble. "I wanted to tell you before you heard from anyone else."

Serena and Sam offered sympathy and condolences.

"Even though it was inevitable, it's still a shock," he said.

A woman got up from the sofa behind Franc and came toward the screen. "I don't know what we're going to do without him!" she wailed.

"This is my sister, Beryle," said Franc.

"We all loved him so much," sobbed Beryle. "Losing him is so hard!"

Murmurs of agreement came from behind them.

"It was good that I could be here for him at the end," Franc said, seeking to regain control of the conversation. Even though his relationship with his father had been difficult, his return home had come at the insistence of his feisty lama, Geshe Wangpo. One of the senior most lamas at Namgyal Monastery, Geshe Wangpo was uncompromising on the importance of actions over words and others over self.

"I'm glad that Geshe Wangpo persuaded me," Franc continued. "My father and I were able to resolve . . ."

"We're having a big funeral," interrupted an elderly, disembodied man's voice from behind Franc.

"*Very* big funeral," chimed in someone else, evidently impressed with the scale of it.

"Over two hundred people are coming to say good-bye," added Beryle, looming up in the screen again. "That's the main thing right now, isn't it? We all need closure, all of us."

"Closure," chorused the group behind her.

"Dad wanted something very simple at the crematorium," said Franc.

Beryle was having none of it. "Funerals are for those of us left behind," she declared. "We're a Catholic family. Well"—she looked pointedly at Franc—"most of us are."

"None of that sky-burial stuff," pronounced the same scratchy male voice from behind.

Franc was shaking his head. "I've never suggested . . ."

"That's what you Buddhists believe in, isn't it?" said a wizened, white-haired figure, eyes red and teeth missing, who was homing in on the computer. "Chop people into little pieces and feed them to the vultures? No, sir."

"This is Uncle Mick," Franc said.

Uncle Mick scrutinized the computer screen for a few long moments before rebuking Franc, "They're not Indian!"

"I never said they were," Franc protested gently, but Mick had already turned his back and was shuffling away.

Franc raised his eyebrows pointedly before saying, "I'm hoping to get out to feed birds in the park tomorrow."

Buddhists believe that acts of generosity benefit those who have died, when dedicated by people who have a close karmic connection to the deceased.

"*Birds?*" Beryle was incredulous. "What about *us?*

What about your own flesh and blood? Plenty of time for that sort of nonsense after the funeral."

"I'd better go," Franc said quickly. "I'll call again when I'm alone."

As Serena and Sam said good-bye, Uncle Mick's voice rose. "Birds? I knew it! There'll be no sky burial as long as I'm around!"

After the call ended, Sam and Serena turned toward each other.

"Looks like he's having a rough time," said Serena.

Sam nodded. "At least he knows he did the right thing by going home. Though he could be back a lot sooner than everyone thought," added Sam, his expression thoughtful.

"Who knows?" Serena ran her fingers through her hair. "If he has to deal with the estate he could be there for a while yet."

Sensing a movement she looked down to find Marcel, Franc's French bulldog, at her feet.

"How did *he* know?" she wondered, smiling at Sam.

"Heard his voice?"

"From under the counter?" She looked over at the dogs' basket. It seemed unlikely that the sound of Franc's voice had traveled that far.

"No," she said, kneeling down to pat him. "I think dogs can sense these things. Can't you, my little friend?"

Soon after that came alarming news much closer to home, news that struck at the very heart of

Namgyal—more specifically, at the office where I over-saw the activities of the Dalai Lama's executive assistants. There was usually something going on in there that I would observe from on top of the filing cabinet behind Tenzin, which offered a panoramic view not only of the office itself but also of everyone who came and went from His Holiness's quarters. Consequently, when the Dalai Lama was out of town, I spent many of my days in the office, watching the to and fro of official business at Jokhang.

Chogyal and Tenzin tried to take their vacations during His Holiness's lengthier absences, and on this occasion it had been Chogyal's turn for time off. Several days earlier he had left to visit family in Ladakh. Two days ago, Chogyal had contacted Tenzin with an urgent message for Geshe Wangpo. With customary efficiency, Tenzin had immediately summoned two novice monks who were undertaking cleaning chores down the corridor.

I had known Tashi and Sashi from my earliest days in the world, when their treatment of me had been shabby, to say the least. Since then they had made great efforts to redeem themselves and were now fervent in their con-cern for my well-being.

"I have an urgent message for you to deliver," Tenzin told them as they entered the office.

"Yes, sir!" they replied in unison.

"It's critical you give this to Geshe Wangpo person-ally," Tenzin emphasized, handing a sealed envelope to ten-year-old Tashi, the elder of the two.

"Yes, sir!" Tashi repeated.

"No delay, no diversion," said Tenzin sternly, "even if you are called by a senior monk. This is official business of His Holiness's office."

"Yes, sir," the boys chorused, their faces glowing with the importance of their unexpected mission.

"Go, now," Tenzin commanded.

They turned to each other briefly, before Tashi said in a piping voice, "Just one question, sir."

Tenzin raised his eyebrows.

"How is HHC, sir?"

Tenzin turned to where I lay sprawled on the filing cabinet. I blinked my eyes open, just the once.

"As you can see, still alive." His tone was droll. "Now hurry!"

No sooner was I back from the café that afternoon and up on the filing cabinet giving my charcoal ears a quick wash than who should appear on the other side of the office but Geshe Wangpo himself. Geshe Wangpo was not only one of Namgyal Monastery's most revered lamas but also one of its most intimidating. An old-school Geshe—the title refers to the highest academic degree for Buddhist monks—he was in his late 70s and had studied in Tibet before the Chinese invasion. He had the round, muscular build typical of a Tibetan, as well as a penetrating intellect and little tolerance for slothfulness of body or mind. He was also a monk of immense compassion, whose love for his students was never doubted.

Such was Geshe Wangpo's commanding physical presence that the moment he appeared at the door, Tenzin rose from his chair and greeted him, "Geshe-la!"

The lama waved for him to sit down. "Thank you for your message two days ago," Geshe Wangpo said, his expression grave. "Chogyal was seriously ill."

"So I heard," said Tenzin. "He was fine when he left here. Perhaps he picked up something on the bus?"

Geshe Wangpo shook his head. "It was his heart." He didn't elaborate. "He deteriorated overnight. He was much weaker but remained conscious. When I called him again early this morning, however, he was unable to speak and barely alive. Unfortunately for us, his time had come. He couldn't move, but he could hear my voice. His physical death was at nine o'clock, but he remained in clear light for more than five hours."

It took Tenzin—and me—the longest time to digest this news. Chogyal, our Chogyal, dead? He had been bustling around this office only three days ago. And still so young: he couldn't have been much older than 35.

"He had a very good death," said Geshe Wangpo. "We can be confident that his continuum has moved forward in a positive direction. Even so, there will be special prayers in the temple tonight, and you may find it useful to make offerings."

Tenzin nodded. "Of course."

As Geshe Wangpo looked from Tenzin to me and back again, his usually stern demeanor softened into an expression of great tenderness. "It is natural to feel sadness, grief, when we lose someone we care for. And Chogyal was a very, very kind man. But you do not have to feel sorry for Chogyal's sake. He lived well. Even though death came unexpectedly, he had nothing to fear. He died well, too. He set a good example for us all."

With that, Geshe Wangpo turned and left the office.

Tenzin leaned forward in his chair and closed his eyes for a while, then got up and came over to the filing cabinet. He reached up and stroked me. "It's hard to believe, isn't it, HHC?" His eyes welled with tears. "Dear, kind Chogyal."

A short while later Lobsang appeared. He crossed the room to where Tenzin was still stroking me. "Geshe-la just told me the news," he said. "I am very sorry."

The two men embraced, Lobsang in his monk's robes, Tenzin in his dark suit. As they separated, Lobsang said, "Five hours in the clear light!"

"Yes, that's what Geshe-la said."

The process of dying is the subject of detailed preparation in Tibetan Buddhism. I often heard His Holiness talk about clear light as the natural state of our mind when it's free of all thought. Because it is a state beyond concept, words can only point to the experience of it; they cannot describe the indescribable. But the words sometimes used to suggest this state are *boundless, radiant, blissful.* It is a state imbued with love and compassion.

Seasoned meditators can experience clear light while still alive, so that when death comes, instead of fearing the loss of their personal identity, they are able to abide in this state of blissful nonduality. With such a level of control that it is possible to direct the mind to what happens next, rather than being propelled by the force of habitual mental activity, by karma.

Even though someone has been declared dead from a medical point of view, while abiding in a state of clear light their body remains supple and their healthy coloring remains. There is no putrefaction of the body or loss of body fluids. To others, it looks as if the deceased is simply asleep. Great yogis have been known to remain in clear light for days, even weeks.

Geshe Wangpo's assurance that Chogyal had been able to abide in the clear light was therefore news of the utmost significance. His life may have been short, but what he had done with it was beyond measure: he would be able to assume some control over his destiny.

Tenzin reached into his drawer, taking out a mobile phone and putting it in his pocket—always a prelude to his leaving the office.

"I'm going to feed some birds," he told Lobsang.

"Good idea," the other monk said. "I'll come with you, if I may."

The two of them walked toward the door.

"That's the main thing right now, isn't it?" observed Lobsang. "Doing whatever we can to help the one who has left us."

Tenzin nodded. "And even if he doesn't need our help so much, it is good to have something positive to focus on."

"Exactly," agreed Lobsang. "Something instead of oneself."

The sound of their voices retreated as they made their way down the corridor. I was left alone on the filing cabinet, thinking about the fact that I would never see Chogyal again. He would never walk through the door, sit in the chair opposite Tenzin, and take out the yellow highlighter that he thought was a pen for marking documents, but I knew was really a toy that could be flicked from the desktop onto the carpet.

I thought, too, about the last time Chogyal had held me, and I had stuck my claws into his arm. Unhappy with him for removing the beige blanket and with it the last evidence of my daughter, I had been mean and miserable. It was not the last memory of me I would have wanted him to have, but it was too late to change. I could only console myself with the knowledge that most of our time together had been happy. When karma drew us together in a future life, as it had in this one, the energy between us would be positive.

From the sill that evening I watched the Namgyal monks make their way across the courtyard alongside the townspeople streaming through the monastery gates. I hadn't realized that the prayers for Chogyal were open to the public, or how well-known and well-loved Chogyal had been in the community.

As more and more people arrived, I decided that I, too, would attend. I made my way downstairs and across the courtyard, and it wasn't long before I was ambling up the temple steps with a group of elderly nuns.

There is something especially magical about the temple at night. And that night, the large statues of Buddha at the front of the temple, with their beautiful, gold-painted faces, were illuminated by a sea of flickering butter lamps, every one dedicated for the benefit of Chogyal and all living beings. Other traditional offerings—food, incense, perfume, and flowers—were part of the same feast of the senses that made my whiskers tingle with delight.

I looked around at the great wall *thangkas* with their vivid depictions of deities like Maitreya, the Buddha of the future; Manjushri, the Buddha of wisdom; Green Tara; Mahakhala, the Dharma protector; the Medicine Buddha; and the revered teacher Lama Tsongkhapa. In the subdued nighttime lighting, the figures seemed somehow closer than during the day, hovering presences looking down from their lotus thrones.

I had seldom seen as many people in the temple as were there that night. From the elderly lamas and rinpoches sitting at the front to the other monks and nuns and the townspeople seated farther back, they took up every available space. One of the nuns I had arrived with found a place for me on a low shelf at the back of the temple from which I could survey everything that happened. People lit butter lamps, brought their hands together in prayer, and murmured to one another in low voices, giving the evening a powerful sense of occasion. Yes, there was a feeling of loss, of course, and deep sadness but another, quite different undercurrent as well. Word of Chogyal remaining in clear light had obviously gone out, and amid the grief there was a quiet pride, even celebration, that he had had such a good death.

Geshe Wangpo's arrival was greeted with an immediate, awed hush. He took his place on the teaching throne—the raised seat at the front of the temple—and led the assembled in a chant before guiding us in a short meditation. There was silence in the temple but not stillness. Rather, a curious energy seemed to pervade the space. Was it just my feline sensitivity that felt the power of hundreds of minds focused on Chogyal's well-being? Could the collective intention of so many accomplished meditators who knew Chogyal so well reach out and benefit him at this very moment?

Geshe Wangpo ended the meditation with the gentle chiming of a bell. After reading a short message from the Dalai Lama, who had sent his personal condolences and special blessings from America, he talked about Chogyal in the traditional Tibetan way, speaking about his family in Kham, a province in Eastern Tibet, and the monastic studies he had begun at an early age, then reciting some of the key teachings Chogyal had received.

Geshe Wangpo was always scrupulous about following tradition. But he also knew how to reach an audience, many of whom were not monastics but ordinary householders. "Chogyal was only thirty-five when he died," he said softly. "If we are to learn anything from his death, and I have no doubt he would want us to, we should realize that death can strike any of us at any moment. Most of the time we don't want to think about this. We accept that death will happen, of course, but we think of it as something that will happen far in the future. This way of thinking"—Geshe Wangpo paused for emphasis—"is unfortunate. Buddha himself said that the most important meditation of all is on death. It is not morbid, not depressing to contemplate one's own death. Completely the opposite! It is only when we have faced the reality of our own death that we really know how to live.

"Living as though we are going to go on forever—this is a tragic waste," he continued. "One of my students, a lady who suffered from stage four cancer, came very close to death last year. When I visited her in the hospital, she was just a frail shadow in a bed, hooked up to all kinds of tubes and equipment. Happily, however, she succeeded in her battle against the disease. And just recently she told me something very interesting: the disease had been the greatest gift she had ever received, she said, for the first time she truly faced her own death—and only then did she realize how precious it is simply to be alive."

Geshe Wangpo paused to allow his message to sink in.

"Now she wakes up every day with a sense of profound gratitude to be here now, free of disease. Every day for her is a bonus. She is more content and at peace with herself. She doesn't worry so much about material things, knowing that these are of only limited, short-term value. She has become a very enthusiastic meditator because she knows from direct experience that whatever happens to her body, consciousness remains.

"The practices given to us in the Dharma help us take charge of our consciousness. Instead of being victims of mental agitation and habitual patterns of thinking, we have a precious opportunity to free ourselves and realize the true nature of our mind. *This* we can take with us. Not our friends, not our loved ones, not our possessions. But awakening to the reality of consciousness as boundless, radiant, and beyond death is an enduring achievement. And with that awareness we realize we have nothing to fear from death." A mischievous smile appeared on his face. "We discover that death, like everything in life itself, is merely a concept."

Geshe Wangpo raised a hand to his heart. "I wish that all of my students could nearly die. There is no better wake-up call on how to live. Perhaps some students, like Chogyal, do not need this. He was a most diligent practitioner, with a warm heart and the incredibly good karma to work closely with His Holiness for some years. Those of us who have the benefit of contact with His Holiness should not underestimate this."

I wondered if Geshe-la was addressing this last comment to me. Sometimes when I heard him in the *gompa,* the monastery, it seemed that much of what he was saying was directed specifically at me. As the being who spends more time with the Dalai Lama than almost any other, what did that say about *my* karma?

"We will continue to remember Chogyal in our prayers and meditations, especially for the next seven weeks," Geshe Wangpo continued, referring to the maximum period during which it is thought that consciousness remains in the *bardo,* the state between the end of one existence and the start of another. "And we should thank him, in our hearts, for reminding us that life is tenuous and may end at any time," he emphasized.

"In the Dharma we have the term *realization*. A realization is when our understanding of something deepens to the point that it changes our behavior. I hope that Chogyal's death helps us all come to the realization that we, too, will die. Such a realization helps us to let go a little, to experience deep appreciation, even awe, just to be alive. We cannot procrastinate with our Dharma practice: time is precious and we must use it wisely.

"Those of us here tonight are among the most fortunate in the world, because we know the practices that can help transform consciousness and our experience of death itself. If we are as dedicated as Chogyal, when death comes, we will have nothing to fear. And while we are still alive . . . how wonderful!"

The next morning, while sitting on the sill, I noticed Tenzin crossing the courtyard half an hour earlier than usual. Instead of making his way straight to the office as he typically did, he went to the temple, where he started the day with a meditation session.

Other changes soon followed. One day he arrived at work carrying a strange-shaped case, which he leaned against the wall behind where Chogyal used to sit. I sniffed it curiously, wondering what it could possibly contain. It was bigger than a laptop-computer case but narrower than a briefcase, with a peculiar bulge on one side.

At lunchtime Tenzin retired to the first-aid room, where he usually ate a sandwich while we listened to the BBC World Service. On this day, however, the most peculiar range of burbles and squeaks sounded from behind the closed door, along with much reedy huffing and puffing. Later I heard him tell a curious Lobsang, "I've had that saxophone sitting at home for the past twenty years. I've always wanted to learn how to play it. One thing I've learned from Chogyal . . ." He nodded toward the chair in which Chogyal used to sit.

"No time like the present," agreed Lobsang. "Carpe diem!"

And me, dear reader? Having no aspirations to play the saxophone or even the piccolo, I didn't plan on giving up my lunchtime visits to the Himalaya Book Café. But Chogyal's death had been an urgent reminder: Life is finite; every day is precious. And simply to wake up in good health truly is a blessing, because sickness and death can strike at a moment's notice.

Even though I had known this before—it was, after all, a theme His Holiness often spoke about—there is a big difference between accepting an idea and changing your behavior. I had been complacent before, but now I realized that each day of good health and freedom was another day in which to create the causes and conditions for a happier future.

Boredom? Lethargy? They seem so irrelevant when remembering how quickly time passes. I understood with stark clarity that for a truly happy and meaningful life, it is necessary first to face death. Authentically, not just as an idea. Because after that, the twilight skies are never so resplendent, the curls of incense never so mesmerizing, the smoked salmon morsels garnished with *Dijonnaise* sauce down at the café never so lip-smackingly, whisker-tinglingly, tail-swishingly delicious.

CHAPTER FIVE

It was about 35 nights into the 49 for which His Holiness was scheduled to be away that I realized something had gone missing from my life. It had slipped away so gradually that I hadn't noticed its absence until it had disappeared almost entirely: I had stopped purring.

I would still purr when Tenzin turned his attention from the marginally important correspondence with world leaders lodged inside the filing cabinet to the far more significant being lying on top of it. And I was also unfailing in signaling my appreciation of the delicious meals served at the Himalaya Book Café.

But apart from this sporadic incidental purring, I had remained mute for most of the past week. And it was doing me no good. Which brings me back to the central question of my investigations: *Why do cats purr?*

The answer may seem perfectly obvious, but as with most other feline activities, it is more complex than it appears. Yes, we purr because we're content. The warmth of a hearth, the intimacy of a lap, the promise of a saucer of milk—all of these may prompt our laryngeal muscles to vibrate at an impressive rate.

But contentment is not the only trigger. Just as a human may smile when she's feeling nervous or because she wants to appeal to your better nature, so cats may purr. A visit to the vet or a trip in the car may prompt us to purr to reassure ourselves. And should your footsteps in the kitchen lead you almost but not quite to the only cupboard of feline interest, you may well hear a throaty purr as we curl a tail suggestively around your leg or plead with a more imperative swishing around your ankles.

Bioaccoustical researchers will tell you something else fascinating: the frequency of a cat's purr is ideal therapy for pain relief, wound healing, and bone growth. We cats generate healing sound waves much the way electrical stimulation is used increasingly in medicine, except that we do it naturally and spontaneously for our own benefit. (Note to cat lovers: Should your darling feline seem to be purring much more than usual, perhaps it's time to pay a visit to the vet. She may know something about her health that you do not.)

But apart from these reasons for purring there is another reason—arguably the most important reason of them all. Just how important I hadn't realized until Sam Goldberg left his door open by mistake.

Few things are more intriguing to a cat than the discovery of a door, hitherto resolutely shut, that has now been left ajar. The opportunity to explore unknown, even forbidden territory is one that we are powerless to resist—which is why I got waylaid late one afternoon when I was about to make my way back to Jokhang. Hopping down from the magazine rack, I noticed that the door behind the bookstore counter was open, and I revised my plans. I knew that the door led upstairs to Sam's apartment. When Franc had hired Sam to set up and manage the bookstore, the deal they struck included Sam's use of the apartment, which until then had functioned as a storage area.

Without hesitation I slipped through the crack in the door, immediately encountering a flight of stairs. They were steep and narrow, covered with musty carpet, and would take a while to climb. But ignoring the stiffness in my hips, I pressed on toward the light issuing from a second door at the top of the stairs. Also ajar, it led into Sam's flat.

I often wondered what Sam got up to when he went upstairs, because from my vantage point, his working life seemed rather dull. While he spent part of each day talking to customers, or opening fresh consignments from publishers, or rearranging the books on display, most of the time he remained behind the counter, glued to his computer. Exactly what he was working on was a mystery. When speaking to Serena, he sometimes used terms like *inventory program, publishers' catalogs,* and *accounting package.* And he often joked about being a geek, liberated the moment he sat behind a keyboard.

But for all those hours? Every day? That made me all the more curious about what I would discover at the top of the stairs.

There was no question that Sam had an interesting mind. People often pronounced him an amazing thinker after a conversation in which they had discussed subjects like the spontaneous manifestation of Tibetan symbols on cave walls, or the similarities between the biographies and teachings of Jesus and Buddha. I wondered if his apartment would be similarly engaging.

I was still mulling over the possibilities when I finally reached the top of the stairs. Realizing that my appearance would be unexpected, I inched forward carefully. Squeezing through the gap between the door and the doorjamb, I found myself in a large, sparsely furnished room. The stark white walls were bare, devoid of pictures. On the left side of the room there was a double bed covered with a faded blue duvet. On the wall to the right were two windows with wooden Venetian blinds. Against the wall opposite the door was a desk with three large computer monitors. Sam was sitting at the desk with his back to me. The floor around him was covered with a tangle of cables and computer equipment.

So *this* was how Sam spent his evenings? Exchanging a seat in front of the screen downstairs for a seat in front of another? There was a beanbag chair in one corner of the apartment. But from the looks of things, most of Sam's time was spent at the computer. Right now he was involved in a video conference call, and there were thumbnail images of the other participants on the monitor screens. I'd heard him explain to Serena that this was one way he kept up with authors, managing sometimes to coax any who were traveling through India to visit the store for a talk or a book signing.

With Sam engrossed in video conferencing, I glanced around the room. My attention was drawn to a cluster of small, round, neon-yellow objects that I instantly recognized from the sports segment on TV: golf balls! Beside them, resting against the door frame, was a putter.

Stealthily I crept toward the balls. When I was a short distance away I crouched down in the stance of a jungle beast and then pounced on the balls, sending one skating across the floor at high speed. It hit the baseboard on the opposite wall with a sharp *thwack.*

Sam spun around and caught me with my paws wrapped around another ball and my mouth open as if to take a bite.

"Rinpoche!" he called out, looking from me to the open door. I flicked away the ball and scampered around the room in a mad frenzy before leaping onto his bed.

He grinned.

"What's happening?" a voice said from one of the speakers.

Sam trained his camera on me for a moment. "Unexpected visitor."

From around the world came a chorus of ooh-ing and ah-ing.

"I didn't know you were into cats," said a man with an American accent.

Sam shook his head. "Not as a rule, but this one is rather special. You see, she's the Dalai Lama's Cat."

"And she visits *you* in *your home*?" someone asked, incredulous.

"Totally awesome!" exclaimed another.

"She's adorable," cooed yet another.

There was great excitement for a few moments as everyone took time to digest this globally significant news. Once normal conversation had resumed, I returned to the golf balls. I hadn't realized how reassuringly solid they were. And such heft! I now knew why golfers could send them flying long distances.

I flicked another ball across the floor toward a black plastic cup. It overshot its mark, hit the baseboard, and came hurtling back toward me. Startled, I leapt aside just in time. Apparently, golfing could be unpredictable and dangerous in ways I had never imagined.

Bored with golf, I wandered down a corridor to find the kitchen. Unlike the kitchens at Jokhang, which were in constant use and in which an enticing medley of scents could always be detected, Sam's kitchen was sterile and uninteresting, probably because he ate most of his meals downstairs. I noticed a few empty beer cans and an ice cream carton in the garbage. No intrigue here.

I was wandering around looking for more rooms— there weren't any—as someone on the conference call was saying, "Psychology is still a young science. It was just over a hundred years ago that Freud coined the term *psychoanalysis*. Since then most of the focus has been on helping people with serious mental challenges. It's only recently that we've seen trends like Positive Psychology, in which the focus is not on going from minus ten to zero but from zero to plus ten."

"Maximizing our potential," chimed in someone.

"A state of greatest flourishing," added someone else.

"What I don't get," Sam was saying, "is why, after all the research in recent decades, there still doesn't seem to be a formula for happiness."

I paused. *Formula for happiness?* That was so Sam, with his programs and codes and algorithms. As if happiness could be reduced to a collection of scientific data.

"There *is* an equation," the man in the center of Sam's screen was saying. "But like most formulas, it needs some explaining."

Really? I wasn't sure if the Dalai Lama knew of such a formula, but the very idea that such a thing might exist made me prick up my ears.

"The formula is H equals S plus C plus V," said the man, as he keyed it in and it came up on the screen. "Happiness equals what's called your *biological set point,* or S, plus the conditions of your life, C, plus V, your voluntary activities. According to this theory, each individual has a set point, or average level of happiness. Some people are naturally upbeat and cheerful, putting them at one end of the bell curve. Others are temperamentally gloomy and fall to the other end. The vast majority of us fall somewhere in the middle. This set point is our personal norm, the base level of subjective well-being we tend to return to after the triumphs and tragedies and day-to-day ups and downs of our lives. Winning the lottery might make you happier for a while, but the research shows that eventually you are likely to revert to your set point."

"Is there a way to change the set point?" asked a young woman with a British accent. "Or are we just stuck with it?"

I hopped from the floor to the bed, and the bed to the desk, so I could follow the discussion better.

"Meditation," said a man with a shiny bald head and glowing skin. "It has a powerful impact. Studies have shown that the set points of experienced meditators are right off the scale."

Yes, I thought, *His Holiness certainly knows about that!*

"Turning to conditions, C," continued the man who had been explaining set-point theory, "there are some things about our conditions we can't control—gender, age, race, sexual orientation, for example. Depending on where you're born in the world, those factors may or may not have a huge impact on your likely level of happiness.

"As for V, the voluntary variables," he said, "these include activities you choose to pursue, such as exercising, meditating, learning to play the piano, getting involved with a cause. Such activities require ongoing attention, which means that you don't habituate to them in the way that you might get used to a new car, say, or a new girlfriend and lose interest when the novelty wears off."

This prompted chuckling around the world.

He went on. "When you take the happiness formula overall, you can see that while there are certain things that can't be changed, there are others that can. The key focus should be on things you can change that will have a positive impact on your feeling of well-being."

A distant crash of cymbals and the blast of a Tibetan horn reminded me of the ceremony being held at Namgyal Monastery that day. All the monks were being treated to a celebratory meal in honor of several newly graduated Geshes who had successfully come to the end of their 14 years of study. In the past, I had found that spending time near the monastery kitchens on such occasions proved very rewarding.

Hopping down from Sam's desk and heading toward the stairs, I reflected on the happiness formula. It was an interesting perspective, and not so different from what His Holiness used to say. Contemporary research from the West and ancient wisdom from the East seemed to be arriving at the same place.

Several days later Bronnie Wellenksy arrived at the café with a new flyer to be posted on the notice board. Bronnie, the 20-something Canadian coordinator of an education charity, used the café notice board to display posters for tourists, announcing activities like visits to craft centers and concerts by local performers. She was boisterous, jolly, and always on the move, her shoulder-length hair perennially disheveled. Although she had been in Dharamsala for only about six months, she was already remarkably well connected.

"This one's perfect for you," she called out to Sam, as she pinned a flyer to the board.

Sam looked up from his screen.

"What's that?"

"We need volunteer teachers to give local teenage kids basic computer training. It boosts their employability."

"I already have a job," replied Sam.

"It's *very* part time," Bronnie said. "Like two evenings a week. Even one evening would be great."

Having secured the flyer in a prominent position, she made her way across to the bookstore counter.

"I've n-never taught anybody before," Sam told her. "I mean, I'm not qualified. I wouldn't know where to begin."

"At the beginning," she shot back, responding to his uncertain expression with a dazzling smile. "It doesn't matter that you've never taught before. These kids know nothing. They don't come from families with computers at home. *Anything* you could help them with would be so, like, amazing. Sorry, I don't know your name," she said, reaching her hand across the counter. "I'm Bronnie."

"Sam."

As he shook her hand, he seemed to notice her for the very first time.

"I've seen you working at the computer," she said.

He held up his arms in mock surrender. "A geek."

"Didn't mean it that way," she said cheerily.

"But it's true,'" he countered, with a shrug.

Holding his gaze she said, "You have no idea how much you could help these kids. Even the stuff you take for granted would be a revelation."

I knew the most likely cause of Sam's reluctance. In the past he had told both Franc and Geshe Wangpo that he just wasn't "a people person." And here was Bronnie asking him to stand up in front of a group and teach.

Bronnie hadn't taken her eyes off his and was still smiling warmly. "Of all the voluntary activities you could do, this would use your abilities best of all."

It was the V word that did it. *Voluntary*. Little did Bronnie know that she had hit on one of the key variables in the happiness formula.

"I would help, of course," she offered.

Could she see his resistance beginning to crack?

"The Internet people across the road are donating their facilities," Bronnie explained. "It would only be one hour, in the late afternoon. Basic word processing, perhaps spreadsheets—that kind of thing."

Sam was nodding.

"Oh, *please* say you'll do it!" she gushed.

A smile formed at the corner of Sam's mouth. "Okay, okay!" he said, looking down at the counter. "I'll do it."

Sam took his teaching responsibilities very seriously. He had soon downloaded some tutorials for beginners, watched some YouTube videos on Teaching 101, and had begun making notes. Several times during quiet moments in the café I heard him asking the waiters about this word or that concept: was it something that young Indians would understand?

I don't know when Sam's first computer skills class took place. It must have been one afternoon after I had already gone home to Jokhang. But soon a perceptible change came over him. He was spending less time behind the counter in the bookstore and more time talking to customers. Something about his posture had changed, too. He looked taller somehow.

His early classes had gone well enough for him to continue. I knew this from a remark Bronnie made when she came to visit him at the café one morning.

"You were *amazing* last night," she told him, her eyes sparkling.

"Oh, it was only . . ."

"Two hours of questions!" she said, laughing. "That's unheard of."

"Everyone seemed to be enjoying themselves."

"Including the geek who can't teach?"

"Even him."

"*Especially* him, I'd say." Leaning over the counter she took his hand and told him something that made him explode with laughter. Yes, Sam—belly-laughing. I wouldn't have believed it myself if I hadn't heard it with my own charcoal ears.

Something was up, dear reader. Something that began with V but didn't end there. Not if my feline intuition was anything to go by.

It was at the end-of-the-day hot-chocolate session that my instincts were confirmed. As it happened, Lobsang was also in the bookstore that evening. Serena asked him to join them, an invitation he accepted. Watching Lobsang and Serena sit down on a sofa side by side, Sam opened the door leading up to his apartment. There was a thundering on the staircase as he ascended. Muffled voices could be heard from above, then the sound of his footsteps descending, followed by those of someone else.

I stared at Bronnie, fascinated. It was the first time I'd seen her with her hair straight and shiny and her face transformed by makeup. She was dressed in figure-hugging jeans and a pretty top.

"This is Bronnie," Sam said, introducing her to Lobsang. No introduction to Serena was needed as they had already met. "My girlfriend," he added.

Bronnie gazed at him with an adoring expression.

Sam beamed.

Lobsang folded his palms together at his heart and bowed.

Serena chuckled. "I'm very happy for both of you!"

After they all sat down, Kusali enacted the end-of-the-day ritual of hot chocolate, dog biscuits, and my saucer of milk.

Lobsang looked from Bronnie to Sam with a serene smile. "So where did you two meet?"

"I needed volunteers for our computer training

program," replied Bronnie. "We're trying to get some of the kids here job-ready, and Sam stepped up to the plate."

Sam grinned. "That's one way of putting it. She wasn't taking 'no' for an answer."

"You can stop any time you like," she teased. Then, looking over at Serena and Lobsang, she said, "He's not going to. He's an amazing teacher, and the kids just love him."

Sam looked down at the floor.

"They even have a name for him."

"Stop!" Sam said.

"The second, or was it the third, evening he was there—"

"Bronnie!"

"—they decided he should be called *Super-Geek.* With the greatest affection, of course."

Serena laughed. "Of course."

Bronnie was relentless. "He has such a great way of getting things across. You can see the lightbulbs going on just like that," she said, snapping her fingers.

"I'm only following online course notes," Sam protested. He felt the need to temper her enthusiasm, although as he leaned back in the sofa he seemed to be enjoying the attention.

"More important than the technical stuff," continued Bronnie, reaching over to take his hand, "you give them confidence. The feeling that whatever they don't know, they can easily master. That's priceless."

"Then you have discovered a real vocation," observed Lobsang.

Sam nodded. "I have. I mean, I love books, but I find I enjoy teaching, too. It's like a whole new dimension has opened up, thanks to Bronnie."

"You mean, thanks to the Formula," she said wryly.

"Formula?" asked Serena.

"Sam says he only started because I was so pushy," Bronnie said. "But then he admitted that voluntary activity was part of some formula for happiness."

"This is most interesting," Lobsang said. "Please tell us about it, Sam."

Sam began explaining about set points, conditions, and voluntary variables. I finished my milk, washed my face, and hopped onto Serena's lap, kneading it tentatively a few times before settling down.

After Sam had finished explaining—with much greater authority than he had explained things in the past—Lobsang said, "So for you, your V—voluntary activity—is helping students get jobs?"

Sam nodded. "Exactly."

"We've already had one company say they'll take our top three students," said Bronnie.

"This is a marvelous example!" Lobsang said, clapping his hands together in delight. "What I like is that by benefiting others, you"—he gestured to Sam and Bronnie as a couple—"have benefited, too! I know a verse that seems relevant. It's about work becoming love made visible."

He began to recite:

"It is to weave the cloth with threads drawn from your heart,

Even as if your beloved were to wear that cloth.

It is to build a house with affection,

Even as if your beloved were to dwell in that house.

It is to sow seeds with tenderness and reap the harvest with joy,

Even as if your beloved were to eat the fruit."

"That's really beautiful, Lobsang," Serena said, gazing at him with affection. "Milarepa?" she asked, citing a Buddhist sage famous for his verse.

Lobsang shook his head. "Kahlil Gibran. I love his poetry." A faraway look came into his eyes as he contemplated the transcendent words he had just quoted.

"He's a favorite of mine, too," agreed Sam. "An interesting choice for a Buddhist monk." Responding to the inquiring expressions around the table, he added, "A lot of Gibran's work is romantic, sensual."

"Yes," Lobsang mused. After a pause, he said, "Sometimes I lose myself in his poetry and forget that I am a this or a that. By the end I am thinking that perhaps being a monk is not necessary."

His words came as an unexpected admission. For the first time he seemed curiously vulnerable.

Serena reached out and squeezed his hand.

From her lap, I looked up at Lobsang and began to purr.

Yes, dear reader, that's the other reason we cats purr. Arguably, it's the most important reason: to make you happy. Purring is our V—our way of reminding you that you are loved and special, and that you should never forget how we feel about you, especially when you're vulnerable.

What's more, purring is our way of ensuring your good health. Studies show that having a feline companion reduces stress and lowers the blood pressure of humans. Cat owners are significantly less likely to have heart attacks than people who live in a catless world.

If you like, you may call this the *science* of purring. While science and art don't always seem to have much to do with each other, in this case they converge in the most life-enhancing way.

As I sat on Serena's lap, my purr growing, I remembered the words of Kahlil Gibran. Had the great poet ever had a feline companion? I wondered. If so, what would he have written about the most important reason that cats purr? Could it have been something along the following lines?

> *It is to heal the body, soothe the mind, and give joy to the heart,*
> *Because it is your beloved's lap that you are sitting on.*

CHAPTER SIX

I was woken from my postlunch siesta by a familiar voice and its usual accompaniment, the percussive sound of a dozen clanging bracelets. Mrs. Trinci was visiting the café with some exhilarating news: "He's come out of retreat!"

She and Serena were standing just a short distance away from me, beside the magazine rack.

"After ten years?" Serena's expression was a mix of astonishment and delight.

"*Twelve*," her mother corrected her.

"Last time I saw him was"—Serena glanced upward, trying to work it out—"before I went to Europe."

"*Sì*," her mother agreed.

"Who told you?" Serena asked.

"Dorothy Cartwright. I dropped in this morning. She's up to her eyes in preparations."

"So he's staying with . . . ?"

"*Sì*, with the Cartwrights!" Mrs. Trinci's eyes gleamed.

"And when will he . . . ?"

"Today!" Mrs. Trinci's cheeks were flushed. "He's on his way from Manali right now!"

The figure at the center of this excitement, I discovered later, was Yogi Tarchin. *Yogi* is not an official title but an informal one he had acquired over the years as his prowess as a meditation master was first affirmed and then increasingly revered. The yogi's inclination toward a meditative life had been evident even when he was a young boy of five or six growing up in the Amdo province of Tibet. Instead of running through the fields with other boys his age, or playing with the wooden toys his father carved, he would take himself off to a small cave in the side of the mountain behind the house and sit on a rock, chanting mantras.

He had undertaken his first extensive retreat in his 20s, secluded from the world for the traditional period of three years, three months, and three days. Since then he had undertaken many more retreats. He had also endured great personal tragedy, losing his wife and two young children during his late 20s, when the bus in which they had been traveling fell down the side of a mountain, killing everyone on board.

Yogi Tarchin's sponsor for his retreats was the Cartwright family of McLeod Ganj, whose daughter, Helen, was a friend of Serena's. Meeting Yogi Tarchin over the tea trolley as a girl of ten, Serena had been instantly drawn to the slight and almost embarrassingly modest man. Even though his English in those days was very limited, it was his presence to which she responded, as so many people did. It was not simply the warmth in his brown eyes but a feeling of timelessness he conveyed, hard to put into words. Around him, one had the sense that the world as we know it is illusory, like clouds passing through the sky, and that behind the appearance is a reality so radiantly expansive that it is breathtaking. It was this reality to which Yogi Tarchin offered a bridge.

Because the Cartwrights and Trincis were good friends, Yogi Tarchin had been entertained by the Trincis at their home. On his return from prolonged periods in Ladakh, Bhutan, or Mongolia, he always made time to see the Trincis, even as his standing as a meditation master grew greater and greater, and long lines of people would form outside his door as monks and lay practitioners from all over the world came to seek instruction or blessings.

Stories about Yogi Tarchin were legendary. There was the time he appeared to one of his students in a dream and was so insistent that the monk visit his aged mother immediately that the very next morning the monk began the two-day trip home to Assam. On arrival he found nothing untoward—his mother was in good health and comfortable in her routine. But on the second day of his visit, a massive storm lashed the whole region, causing flash floods that in turn led to a massive landslide. His mother's house, secure on its hillside for half a century, suddenly jolted free and began a perilous slide to catastrophe. Had the monk not been on hand to protect her, his mother would almost certainly have been killed.

Another story involved a student who had undertaken a three-month solitary retreat in a cave in Ladakh. After he rejoined his monastery, he was asked who had provided him with food. Yogi Tarchin, the monk had replied, when the yogi came to give him regular instruction. This seemed unexceptional until the other monks told him that during those three months Yogi Tarchin hadn't missed a single meditation session with them, in their *gompa* 50 miles away. Without roads or transport, the only way Yogi Tarchin could have covered the distance was through *lung-gom-pa,* a practice by which highly adept practitioners are able to effortlessly cover great distances at super-human speeds.

Then there was the American philanthropist who had collected donations for a school in Tibet that Yogi Tarchin was helping to restore. The benefactor wanted to offer the yogi the donation in person when he visited India four months hence; Yogi Tarchin told him to convert the sum into Australian dollars. Surprised by the instruction but knowing better than to question it, the benefactor followed it to the letter. Over the next three months, the value of Australian currency appreciated by 15 percent, at which point Yogi Tarchin sent a message that the money could now be changed into Indian rupees. The yogi's facility not only for currency exchange but also for language, commerce, and any other mundane activity he chose to engage in was well known. He may not have spent much time in the ordinary world, but he understood it perfectly.

As a layperson, sometimes known as *a householder* in Tibetan Buddhism, Yogi Tarchin needed to sustain himself, and in the past he had taken on the occasional office job between retreats. But his main focus remained on meditation, most recently, four three-year retreats in succession, during which his modest needs had been met by the Cartwrights. No one had seen Yogi Tarchin for more than 12 years. If he had been capable of the most astonishing accomplishments before this period, what more might he have realized by the end of it?

Serena was by no means alone in wondering this, as I discovered on my return to Jokhang. In the executive assistants' office, Tenzin and Lobsang were talking about Yogi Tarchin, too. They didn't know how long he planned to stay in McLeod Ganj, but they would send a letter asking him to stay at least until the Dalai Lama returned. His Holiness would most certainly want to meet with him again.

Over at the temple the next morning, I sat sunning myself as the monks arrived for the late morning meditation session. Several times I heard Yogi Tarchin's name mentioned, along with stories of his amazing powers. That was when I decided I was going to meet the yogi for myself. Hearsay and secondhand reports are all very well, but there's nothing like the direct experience of sitting on a person's lap to get a feeling for what they're really like. Serena had secured an audience with this mystical figure. In her childhood she had been close to both Yogi Tarchin and Buddhism, but her time in Europe had filled her with doubts that had become obstacles to her practice. Not to mention that there were more personal matters on which she wished to seek his advice.

That is how I came to find myself at the Cartwrights' house two days later. Not far from Namgyal Monastery, their home was a rambling old villa with pressed-tin ceilings and polished wooden floors layered with intricately woven Indian rugs. Dorothy Cartwright and I had met numerous times during her visits to the Himalaya Book Café, and while she may have been surprised to find me following closely in Serena's footsteps, she would no sooner have closed the front door in my face than she would have forbidden access to His Holiness himself.

A short while later Serena was slipping off her shoes and softly knocking on a wooden door. I noticed her hands trembling slightly.

Summoned by Yogi Tarchin, she turned the brass door-knob and entered a room that seemed to be from another era. Large and spacious, it was lighted only by three narrow panel windows that glowed like bars of gold, casting an ethereal glow on the low daybed where Yogi Tarchin sat cross-legged. He was wearing a faded crimson shirt, and its muted hue and high, Nehru collar drew attention upward to a face that was as tranquil as it was ageless. When his dark brown eyes met Serena's, his face lit up with such warmth that the air in the room seemed to dance with joy.

Kneeling on the carpet in front of Yogi Tarchin, Serena brought her hands to her heart and bowed deeply. He reached over, clasping her folded hands between his own, and touched his forehead to hers. They remained like that for the longest time, Serena's shoulders shaking and tears sliding down her cheeks.

Finally she sat back and met his gaze of pure compassion. Words were unnecessary as the two of them sat together. Normal conversation was superfluous as they embraced again at a deeper level.

Then Yogi Tarchin spoke. "My dear Serena, you have brought someone with you."

She turned, looking to where I sat just inside the door. "I think she wanted to meet you."

He nodded.

"She is very special," Serena told him.

"I can see."

"She is His Holiness's Cat," Serena explained. "But she's spending a lot of time with us while he's traveling." She paused. "Do you allow . . . ?"

"Not as a rule," he said. "But seeing that she is your little sister . . ."

Little sister? It was said that Yogi Tarchin, like other

realized masters, was clairvoyant. Or was he speaking metaphorically? Whatever the case, I required no further invitation. Launching myself toward him, I hopped up on his daybed and sniffed at his shirt. It smelled of cedar with perhaps a whiff of leather, as though it had been hanging in a cupboard for a very long time.

Just being physically close to Yogi Tarchin was an extraordinary experience. Like His Holiness, he seemed to emanate a particular energy. Along with a sense of oceanic peace he also conveyed a feeling of timelessness, as if this state of exalted wisdom had always existed just as it existed now, and always would exist.

As he asked after Serena's mother, I confirmed that his was a lap I wished to sit on. I settled down on the blanket stretched across his legs, and he stroked me gently. The sensation of his hand against my fur sent a shiver of contentment through my whole body.

"Twelve years is such a long time," Serena was saying. "Four retreats in a row. May I ask why you decided to continue?"

A cuckoo sounded through the late afternoon air.

"Because I could," Yogi Tarchin said simply. Then, seeing Serena's perplexed expression, he added, "It was the most precious opportunity. Who knows when I may encounter such circumstances again?"

She nodded. She was considering the implications of 12 years with no human contact, no TV, radio, newspapers, or the Internet; 12 years with no dining out or entertainment, no birthdays, Christmases, Thanksgivings, or other festivities. Most people would consider such sensory deprivation a form of torture. But Yogi Tarchin had willingly undertaken it, and the transcendental effect on him was palpable.

But another, more negative undertow was troubling Serena. "I suppose as an advanced meditator"—she bowed to Yogi Tarchin—"such training is very useful. But for someone like me . . ." It was as though she couldn't bring herself to express her reservations.

Smiling, Yogi Tarchin leaned forward and touched her hand. "Which is better," he asked, "a doctor or a first-aid worker?"

She looked surprised by the question.

"A doctor," she answered immediately, and then hesitated. "But if someone just needed minor attention . . ."

"Both are useful," he confirmed.

She was nodding.

"To train in first aid takes how long—a few days? But a medical doctor?"

"Seven years. Longer if they specialize," Serena said.

"Is that not a waste of time? Seven years when instead they could be out helping people within days?"

There was a pause while Serena absorbed the real meaning of what he was saying.

"All these meditators," he said, with a gesture that encompassed the Himalaya region and beyond. "Why are they not working for charity? This is how some people think. Much better they help distribute food and build shelter for the homeless instead of sitting on their bottoms all day."

Serena chuckled at this reminder of Yogi Tarchin's direct manner.

"Very good to help humans and animals with charity. This is useful, like first aid. But a permanent solution to suffering requires something different: transformation of the mind. To help others achieve that we must first remove what is obscuring our own mind. Then, like the doctor, our capacity to help is very much greater."

"There are some who would say that this is all just talk," Serena said. She seemed glad for the opportunity to discuss her reservations frankly. "They would say that consciousness is just the brain at work, so the idea of transformation over many lifetimes . . ."

Yogi Tarchin nodded, eyes twinkling. "Yes, yes. The superstition of materialism. But how can something give rise to a quality that it doesn't possess?"

Serena's brow furrowed. "I don't follow."

"Can a stone create music? Can a computer feel sadness?"

"No," she acknowledged.

He nodded once. "Can flesh and blood produce consciousness?"

She reflected on this for a while. "If the brain doesn't create consciousness," she said, "why is it that if the brain is damaged then the mind is also affected?"

Yogi Tarchin smiled broadly and rocked back on his cushion for a moment. "Very good! Very good that you are questioning! Tell me, if your television set is damaged and you can't see anything except a black screen, does it mean that there is no more television?"

As her smile grew, he didn't wait for an answer. "Of course not! Of course, if your brain is damaged it affects the experience of consciousness. Perhaps consciousness cannot be experienced at all. But the brain is only like a receiver, a television set. It's . . . unfortunate to confuse the two.

"If anyone ever says to you, 'Ah, mind is just brain,' then ask them, 'Please tell me where memories are stored.' They will have to admit to you, 'We do not know.' Despite many years of research and much money, scientists have never discovered where in the brain memories are stored. They never will because they are not stored physically! Scientists have done experiments on animals, destroying parts of the brain that they thought contained memory. But the animals could still remember. Neuroscientists, psychologists, philosophers—they all have their ideas about mind. But an idea is just an idea, just a concept. It isn't the thing itself. If we want to know what mind really is, we must experience it firsthand. Directly."

"In meditation?"

"Of course. Some people are frightened to do this. They worry that if they experience a mind free of thought, somehow they will cease to exist. They will disappear in a puff of smoke!" He smiled. "But thoughts are just thoughts. They arise, abide, and pass. When we are able to settle in pristine awareness, free from the thought that has just gone and the one that will arise, we can see our own mind for ourselves. We experience its qualities. Just because it's hard to describe those qualities doesn't mean that the mind doesn't have any."

Serena looked puzzled. "What do you mean?"

"Can you really describe the qualities of chocolate? You can say it is sweet and melts in the mouth and comes in different flavors, but these are just ideas—just concepts pointing to something that is not conceptual in nature. In the same way, we can describe the mind as boundless, radiant, serene, all knowing, loving, and compassionate in nature. But again"—he shrugged—"these are mere words. Verbal fiction."

"I suppose most of us think of body and mind as just this," Serena said, gesturing toward her physical form.

Yogi Tarchin nodded. "Yes. It is a tragic misunderstanding to have such self-limiting beliefs, to think that you are nothing but a bag of bones, rather than boundless consciousness; to believe that death is an ending, not a transition. Worst of all is not to realize how every action of body, speech, and mind affects your future experience of reality, even beyond this time and this life. Beliefs like these make people waste the opportunities of our very precious human life. Our minds are so much greater than this!"

"All-knowing?" Serena asked.

"We have that potential."

"Clairvoyant?"

He shrugged. "Some make a big fuss of this. But clairvoyance arises naturally in an unobstructed mind."

"What about dreams?"

"In a mind that is agitated, untrained, a dream is just a dream—*unless* you have the good fortune to have a teacher who can reach through this agitation."

For a moment he stopped stroking me. I turned my head and looked up at him until he resumed.

"If you are a trained person, sleep offers an amazing opportunity. Knowing that you are dreaming when you're dreaming enables you to control the dream. We can project our consciousness into different realms of experience."

Yogi Tarchin reflected on the common theme underlying Serena's questions before asking, "Why such questions about clairvoyance and dream states?"

She looked down at her hands, which were folded in her lap.

"I think, perhaps, there is something else?" he added.

I saw her cheeks color as she glanced at him briefly. "I guess . . ."

Yogi Tarchin remained silent and perfectly still. The only movement in the room was a silver ribbon of smoke curling lazily upward from a stick of incense burning in the window.

"I got back from Europe just a couple of months ago," Serena began.

"Yes, yes," he confirmed, as though well aware of this and urging her to continue.

"My plan was to come home just for a short break. But being here I've begun to question my reasons for wanting to return to Europe. I think it would be better, and I could be happier, if I stayed here." She met his eye.

"Very good," he said, seeming to affirm the decision.

"But I'm not sure. You see, I'm single. I don't know if Dharamsala is the place. You don't meet the kind of people here . . ."

"I see," he said gently, after her words trailed off. A sparkle of mischief suddenly played across his face. "You want me to be a fortune-teller?"

Serena's smile was rueful. Bringing her palms together at her heart she said, "You have qualities . . ."

"Such prostrating"—he wagged his forefinger—"is not necessary. What arises for you depends on your actions, on the karma and conditions you create."

"Oh." Her mouth fell. "I thought it was possible for you to see the lives of others."

Yogi Tarchin responded to her disappointment. "You have no reason to worry," he told her.

She looked at him beseechingly. "Do you see children

in my future? I'm beginning to think of a very different way of life . . ."

Her words hung suspended in the warmth of the afternoon before Yogi Tarchin told her simply, "You have created the causes for much happiness."

Wordlessly, he communicated a profound sense that all would be well.

Serena sat back, her shoulders relaxing.

For a while their talk turned to how things were going at the Himalaya Book Café and Yogi Tarchin's plans to remain in McLeod Ganj for several months and give teachings. Then the conversation came to a close. As Serena thanked Yogi Tarchin for their time together, he took her hands and thanked her, in turn, for reestablishing the connection.

I hopped off the yogi's lap as Serena got up and followed her across the carpet. The light in the room was even more subdued now—the three panels of gold had turned to silver—but the room was alive with energy. Serena left with the feeling that, at some profound level, all was well and always would be.

Yogi Tarchin followed Serena to the door, then watched as we made our way down the corridor with me padding along behind Serena, my bushy gray tail held high. Serena was just about to turn the corner at the end when he called after her, "Perhaps you have already met him."

She paused, turning around. "You mean, here in Dharamsala?"

He nodded. "I am thinking."

Later, over the end-of-the-day hot chocolate, Serena told Sam, "I so wish everyone could meet Yogi Tarchin. Or someone like him."

Bronnie was taking a class, so it was just the three of us and the dogs.

Serena had been describing her visit with Yogi Tarchin and their conversation. Not the bit about her romantic prospects, of course, but more of what he had been saying about the mind.

"It's not just the explanations, the words," she said. "It's the sensation you have in his presence. This vibe. I can't really describe it, but when you're with him you feel qualitatively different."

Sam was nodding.

"He's living, breathing proof of what happens when we realize the potential of our minds," Serena said, her eyes sparkling. "*Everything* is possible. It goes way beyond even stuff like clairvoyance and telepathy, which occur naturally with an unobstructed mind, Yogi Tarchin says."

"Even ordinary minds are more capable of those sorts of things than most people believe," Sam said.

Serena raised her eyebrows.

"Most people experience telepathy or precognition at some point but just think of them as chance events," he continued. "Coincidence. Most scientists won't even look at evidence for ESP because they believe it's rubbish. Ironically, that's quite an unscientific attitude, because most of them are denouncing the subject without even looking at the evidence." He chuckled. "Interesting how through the ages, when people have shown mystical powers they've been either revered or reviled. A much more sensible reaction, you'd have thought, would be to wonder, how can I, too, develop those powers?"

"Exactly."

"We're innately wired for them." Sam made the assertion with such confidence that Serena raised an eyebrow. Putting down his mug, he stood up and walked to one of the shelves, then pulled out a book and returned with it.

"There are tons of research studies in here, proper clinical trials done by scientists who *are* prepared to investigate things objectively. They show that the so-called paranormal is actually normal. One experiment I like, which has been replicated a number of times, hooks up people to a lie detector as they look at a sequence of images on a computer, either emotionally calm ones like landscapes or shocking ones like corpses cut open for autopsies. A computer randomly selects the images, so that no one, not even the researchers, knows whether the next image will be a calm one or a shocking one. What do you think happens?"

"The needle goes wild every time people are shown a shocking image?"

He shook his head. "Three seconds *before* they're shown a shocking image. Before the computer has even made the selection. It's precognition. And these are just ordinary people being tested."

Serena sat back in her chair with a smile. Having finished my milk, I took the available lap as an invitation.

"The mind isn't just a computer made of meat," said Sam.

"And we're not just human beings capable of spiritual experiences," added Serena, "but also spiritual beings capable of human experiences."

Kneading her legs, I extended my claws through her clothes for just a moment.

She winced before adding, "Or feline experiences."

"Naturally," deadpanned Sam.

That night as I curled up on the bed I usually shared with the Dalai Lama, I contemplated the extraordinary insights into the mind revealed by Yogi Tarchin. And I realized that true happiness is only possible with a panoramic understanding of mind. A limited, bag-of-bones view, as he put it, could only ever yield limited happiness—passing sensory pleasures, temporary contentment, experiences that blaze for a few glorious moments before dying away. But the feeling of profound well-being in people like Yogi Tarchin and His Holiness was so strong you could actually feel it. And it had nothing to do with temporary pleasures: Yogi Tarchin hadn't had any of those for 12 years! No, this feeling was oceanic, enduring, profound—happiness of a very different order.

There is an air of impending danger when His Holiness returns to the room. He is young, in his mid-20s. Accompanying him is an older Tibetan lady with a kind but fearless face. Her brocade shawl is gathered at the neck with a turquoise clasp. She carries herself like a queen.

Following the two are a number of attendant monks, moving urgently about the room. They gather up papers, pack personal items into cases, roll up the intricately woven rugs. I recognize one of them as a very young Geshe Wangpo. They are in a great hurry.

Lying on the sill, I have been looking out of the window of the Potala Palace, across Lhasa to where mountains rise on the other side of the valley. As the Dalai Lama enters the room I lift my head to watch.

Feeling a slight itchiness, I raise my right rear leg reflexively and scratch myself several times. Looking down I see that my leg is short and covered in course, shaggy fur. My tail is also short, with a plume of woolly hair. Instead of retractable claws, my nails are wide and blunt. His Holiness comes over and picks me up. "This is the day we have all feared," he whispers softly in my ear. "The Red Army is invading Tibet. The decision has been made, and I must leave Lhasa as soon as possible. My advance party can't carry you with us through the mountains. It wouldn't be fair to anyone. But Khandro-la will take the very best care of you here in Tibet. She will look after you, as if you were me."

Now I know why the lady with the turquoise clasp has come. There is a moment of intense heartache. Is it emanating from the Dalai Lama or from me?

Turning away, so that it's just the two of us looking out the window and down the valley, His Holiness whispers, "I don't know how long I will have to be away. But I promise I will find you again, my little one." There is a pause before he continues, "Even if not in this lifetime, then definitely in a future one."

As this is happening, I know my dream is a dream.

Only it isn't. I am also being allowed a brief, unobstructed glimpse into my past.

As a dog . . .

CHAPTER SEVEN

ME?!?!

I won't pretend, dear reader, to have been anything but astounded by the dream. However, after the meeting with Yogi Tarchin I had no doubt about the truth of what I had seen. For a few extraordinary moments, I had been able to tune in to a previous experience of consciousness.

Then it was gone.

Waking up early the next morning, I remembered Yogi Tarchin talking about "the good fortune to have a teacher who can reach through this agitation." And I knew that wherever in the world the Dalai Lama happened to be, the dream had been a gift. An affirmation of the bond that drew me to him—a bond, I was startled to discover, that reached back to a previous lifetime.

Perhaps I should not be so amazed. Was it not conventional Buddhist teaching that the law of cause and effect, or karma, spans many lifetimes? The reason why good things happen to bad beings and bad things to good beings doesn't necessarily arise from causes they have created in this particular lifetime. As I had just experienced, only the flimsiest of veils prevents us from reviewing, with perfect clarity, previous moments of consciousness. And what was the passage of a few decades in the context of beginningless time but a momentary leap from one place to another? Nevertheless, the dream opened the door to possibilities I had never considered, such as who I had been in previous lifetimes.

And *what!*

A Lhasa Apso in 1959, it seems, when the Dalai Lama was forced into exile.

The idea that I had been a dog was deeply disconcerting. It certainly put into perspective my woes about the fact that my impeccable Himalayan breeding was undocumented. Bloodlines, pedigree, and so forth suddenly paled in significance compared to the much more important matter of where my consciousness had been, what it had experienced, and what it had done, the effects of which I was experiencing in the here and now. As much as I, like other felines, see our species as altogether superior to canines, one thing I cannot deny is that dogs have consciousness. Like cats and humans they fall into the category of *sem chens,* Tibetan for *mind-havers.*

In the curious way that a number of seemingly unrelated events can sometimes occur around the same time in your life, pointing you toward a single, unmistakable truth, within days of the dream I was eavesdropping on the most intriguing conversation down at the Himalaya

Book Café. The person leading the conversation wasn't one of Sam's book-club speakers, although he was as well-known as the best of them. A biologist from one of Britain's top universities, he was a research fellow whose studies of memory and consciousness had been published in books that were bestsellers worldwide. Visiting McLeod Ganj he just happened to walk past the café. It was 10 A.M., and he decided he was in the mood for a cup of coffee. Stepping inside, he couldn't avoid a large poster of himself above an even larger stack of his latest book. Wearing precisely the same tweed jacket, forest-green shirt, and corduroy trousers as in the photo, he paused to stare at it and then realized that behind the counter, Sam was looking from the poster to him and back again.

Catching each other's eyes, they both laughed.

Then Sam came down the steps, hand extended. "A great honor to have you in the store," he said. "If I'd known . . ."

"I just happened to be walking past," the biologist told him in his clipped English accent. "I didn't know about this place."

"I'm sure you hear this all the time, but I'm a *big* fan of your work!" Sam told him. "I've been following you for years. We have all your books." He gestured to the shelves behind him. "Would you mind signing a few?"

"Delighted," the visitor said.

Sam led him to the counter, grabbing a handful of books on the way and offering him a pen. "If I'd known you were coming to Dharamsala, I would have invited you to speak to our book club."

"Just a flying visit," said the scientist.

Sam pressed on. "So many people here would be fascinated to meet you." As the author worked his way through the pile of books, a thought struck Sam. "I don't suppose you're free at lunchtime today, are you? I could invite a few people."

"I have a meeting at eleven that I expect won't last much more than an hour or so," the biologist said. "After that, as it happens, I'm free for a little while."

By the time the scientist returned there were ten people seated at a table near the bookstore, waiting to have lunch with him. Along with Serena and Bronnie, the group included Ludo and some of his yoga students, Lobsang from Jokhang, and a couple of others I recognized from the book club. As usual, the mood in the café was lively and upbeat; and when the guest arrived, he was welcomed as a much-honored friend. Meals were ordered, drinks poured, and as everyone waited for their food, Sam turned to the biologist and asked, "Are you able to share with us what you're working on at the moment?"

"Certainly," he said. "An avenue of research I've been exploring for many years is the sentience of animals—what consciousness means in nonhuman beings and how it differs from ours."

"Like the way dogs can hear pitches that we can't?" asked one of the book-club members.

"Differences in perception are part of it," offered the guest. "And it's interesting how animals are increasingly being used for their perceptive skills. We're all quite used to guide dogs for the blind, but now we're seeing much broader applications—for example, diabetes service dogs that alert people to hypoglycemia by detecting odor changes in their breath.

"And then," he continued, "there are the marked improvements that have been reported in patients with cerebral palsy, autism, and Down syndrome after direct encounters with dolphins. What is it about these particular creatures that can create such dramatic changes? It has been established that the perceptual consciousness of dolphins is in some ways greatly superior to that of humans. What's more, cetaceans are the only mammals other than humans that clearly demonstrate vocal learning. By better understanding the perceptual and communication powers of dolphins could we develop different treatment modalities for patients with cerebral palsy?"

Sukie from the yoga studio couldn't contain herself. "I heard a story of a woman who had an experience swimming with dolphins. A dolphin kept nudging her in the abdomen, then without warning it flipped her so that she landed on her back on the surface of the water. She was winded but okay, though she was taken to the ER as a precaution. When they did a scan they found a tumor in her stomach exactly where the dolphin had nudged her. Fortunately, it was treatable."

The biologist nodded. "There are many such stories, and part of my work is collecting these in a database and having them properly investigated. As you're suggesting, there are many aspects of nonhuman sentience that go beyond our current understanding but could be extraordinarily useful.

"Animal precognition is well established," the scientist pointed out. "Since the earliest times, people have recorded unusual animal behavior before earthquakes. Wild and domesticated animals become fearful or anxious, dogs howl, birds take flight. A fascinating example was recorded by a biologist studying the mating behavior of toads in San Ruffino Lake in central Italy. He found that the number of male toads in a breeding group fell from more than 90 to almost none within just a few days. Then there was a 6.4 magnitude earthquake followed by aftershocks. The toads didn't return for another 10 days. It appears that days in advance they had detected what was about to happen."

"Earth tremors. Maybe the toads have especially sensitive feet?" someone suggested.

"If so, you would think that seismologists would pick up the same thing," said the scientist. "Maybe there was some subtle change in the electrical field that they picked up. But you know, it's not just toads who have this ability. The big tsunami that hit Asia in December 2004 was anticipated by many different species. There were reports of elephants in Sri Lanka and Sumatra moving to higher ground long before the waves struck, and buffalo doing something similar. Dog owners found that their dogs didn't want to go near the beach for their usual morning walk."

"A tsunami alert system could be created using animals," proposed Ludo.

"I've suggested that myself," the biologist said.

"What if the ability to anticipate earthquakes isn't about seismology or electrical fields?" asked Bronnie. "What if it's some kind of consciousness that animals have?"

"You mean, a survival thing?" chimed in Ludo.

The biologist turned to them both. "You may well be right," he said. "There's evidence that animals have the ability to pick up on things in ways that other people would describe as paranormal. Like the phenomenon of dogs that know when their owners are coming home."

"You wrote a book about that," observed Sam.

"Indeed. There's little doubt that some animals can intuitively detect such things as when their owners are leaving work to come home. There's closed-circuit TV footage showing the dogs getting up and sitting near the front door or a window at exactly the moment their owners leave the office, no matter what time that is. In some cases, dogs have gotten excited about the imminent arrival of someone who had been away from home for days or weeks at a time. There was a merchant marine who would never tell his wife when he was coming home in case he got delayed, but she always knew anyway, because the dog told her."

"I always thought dogs were special that way," announced one of the book-club members.

Lying on the shelf, I bristled. Then I remembered my dream and didn't bristle quite so much.

"As it happens, there are also reports of cats doing the same thing," said the scientist. "There's a wonderful story of a couple who went on a sailing trip for several months, leaving their neighbor to feed the cat. Not even they knew exactly when they'd be returning. But when they came home, they found a loaf of fresh bread and pint of milk waiting for them in their fridge. The neighbors expected them back because for the first time since they'd gone, their cat had gone out to the parking lot in front of their building and spent all day looking up the road."

There were smiles all around the table.

"You could argue that knowing where your next meal is coming from is an important element of survival," the scientist said, glancing at Ludo. "And similarly, there's a lot of data showing that many animals, especially those most at risk from predators, can sense when they're being stared at, which could be critically important to their survival."

"He wrote a book on that, too," announced Sam.

The author laughed.

"There are other elements of animal sentience that go even further. Like the work by Dr. Irene Pepperberg with an African gray parrot called Alex, described in a book I didn't write"—he smiled at Sam—"but which inspired other researchers. It's well understood that parrots have the capacity not only to learn words but also to use them meaningfully. They know the difference between red and green, square and circle, and so on. They also understand, and can communicate, the difference between present and absent.

"Another researcher who had an African gray discovered that the bird seemed to pick up on her thoughts. Once when she picked up the phone to dial her friend Rob, the parrot spontaneously said, 'Hi, Rob.' Another time, she was looking at a picture of a purple car, and the bird, which was upstairs at the time, called out, 'Look at the pretty purple.' Most intriguing of all was the time the bird owner had a dream in which she was using an audio tape deck. The parrot, which slept near her, said out loud, 'You gotta push the button,' as she was about to do that in her dream. He woke her up!"

"Mind reader?" asked Bronnie.

"The parrot was rigorously tested on that. I'm oversimplifying, but basically the bird's responses were recorded as he tried to identify images his owner was looking at in another room. The images were of things like a bottle, a flower, a book, even a naked body. The bird got the naked body right, by the way. In seventy-one trials he averaged twenty-three hits, way more than chance.

"What all of this tells us," the biologist said, "is that nonhuman beings not only share many elements of consciousness with us but also have different perceptual skills that in some cases may be even more subtle than ours."

"More sophisticated," suggested someone.

"That's a value judgment," said the biologist with a smile. "But some would agree. We shouldn't forget, however, that there's much we don't know about human consciousness."

All the while the biologist was speaking, Lobsang had been listening carefully, a serene presence in his red robes. Finally he asked, "Is human consciousness what brings you to McLeod Ganj?"

The scientist nodded. "Buddhism has much to teach the world about the nature of mind: what it is, what it is not, and how theories create divisions in our understanding of consciousness that don't actually exist."

"Mind transcends the world of thought," said Lobsang.

The biologist met his eye with a look of deep recognition. "Quite so. And that simple but profound truth is something that we humans find hard to grasp."

That evening I went to yoga class with Serena. During the past couple of weeks I'd become something of a regular. Rather than sitting alone in an empty apartment, I much preferred to perch on the wooden bench at the studio, listening to Ludo and watching his students work through the sequence of asanas that was becoming more familiar to me. In particular I liked the postclass discussions on the balcony and the warm companionship I felt while sitting on the rug as Serena and the others sipped their green tea, while the mountains enacted their own nightly ritual, their icy caps slowly deepening from white to burnished gold to cerise with the setting sun performing its own salutation.

This evening's class was proceeding in the usual way, the students having worked through standing asanas before taking to their mats for seated twists. In his loose pants and T-shirt, Ludo was walking barefoot around the room, making an adjustment here and a suggestion there as he scrutinized every student's posture in forensic detail.

It was as Ludo was standing with his back to the balcony, talking the class through *Marichyasana III*, the Sage's Pose, that I caught the sudden movement. Behind him on the balcony rail a huge rat appeared, seemingly from nowhere, and paused on Serena's scarf, which as usual she had draped over the rail before coming in to class.

I won't pretend it was the precise location of the rat that made me react the way I did, although I knew how much the scarf meant to Serena. Though faded and worn, the yellow scarf with its embroidered hibiscus blooms was of great sentimental value, being the only gift from her father that she still possessed. I had heard her tell the story of his giving it to her one evening on their balcony at home when she was 12.

The unwelcome sight of a rodent outside provoked a sound I hadn't even known I was capable of. Low and loud, it was a warning of such terrible foreboding that I could see the chill in Ludo's eyes as he looked at me before turning to look outside. By the time he did, the rat had gone. Ludo went out on the balcony, pausing for only a moment before returning swiftly to the room.

"Please, all of you, get up calmly, collect your shoes, and leave the house. There's a fire next door!"

Looking at the tall, youthful Indian man in the second row, Ludo asked, "Sid, could you use that extinguisher from the balcony?"

Sid nodded.

"I'll get another one from the kitchen and come around from the back."

Everyone else rushed to put on their shoes and get out the door. Serena grabbed me on the way. Within moments we were clustered in a group across the road from Ludo's house, stunned by what was happening next door.

Flames were leaping from a window at the front of the house. Dark smoke billowed out, along with the smell of oil. The eaves were already alight. The gap between them and the eaves of Ludo's house was very narrow.

Holding me tightly with one hand, Serena dialed the Dharamsala Fire Department with the other. Several other students hurried into the neighboring house to see what could be done from within. Still others dispersed in search of hoses and buckets of water.

From the corner of the balcony, Sid blasted Ludo's eaves with the fire extinguisher before aiming it at the flames issuing from the kitchen window next door. Ludo raced out the front door of his house with a second extinguisher, just as a fireball exploded through the neighbor's kitchen roof. Ludo focused his spray on the roof, unleashing a forceful blast of foam that made the flames retreat completely, only to burst out, moments later, a short distance away.

Sukie and Merrilee appeared, carrying the end of a garden hose from a house along the road.

"Don't get that anywhere near the kitchen!" Ludo shouted over his shoulder. "This is probably an oil fire. Use the hose to dampen the house walls!" The woman and three children who lived next door were huddled helplessly on the side of the road. With her permission, Ludo headed into her house, seeking the source of the fire. The windows were glowing smoky orange. After two blasts from the fire extinguisher, the orange turned to black.

Out on the balcony, a smoke-smeared Sid was battling the fire on the eaves. The flames were blazing dangerously close to Ludo's roof, and he would no sooner spray them into submission than they would leap back to life. The longer he fought, the weaker the spray coming from the extinguisher. Then it cut out completely. The flames shot up, gaining ground on the neighboring eaves, then leapt effortlessly across to Ludo's house.

Cries of alarm rose from all who had gathered outside. Serena had been told a fire engine would be there in 20 minutes. But by then Ludo's home and the yoga studio would be completely engulfed in flames.

Sid disappeared from the balcony, then emerged from the front door. "We need more extinguishers!" he shouted, looking down the road.

"The others are asking the neighbors," Serena called back. "Two people are driving to the hardware store."

A thunderous explosion inside the neighbor's house was followed moments later by a fireball roaring out the kitchen window and up the side of Ludo's house.

Ludo's efforts inside appeared to be failing, too. He came through the front door waving his extinguisher.

"Empty!" he yelled, quickly crossing the road.

For a moment Ludo and Sid stood staring at the fire. It had firm hold of the neighbors' eaves and roof and had crossed to Ludo's balcony. The students spraying water on the walls of both properties were struggling in vain. In no time the entire roof of the neighboring property would be ablaze, and Ludo's would quickly follow.

A crowd of onlookers had formed, neighbors and passersby who were stunned, anxious, and mesmerized by the conflagration. It felt like an age later but it was probably only minutes before an ancient white Mercedes appeared, tearing up the street toward us, then braking sharply in front of the blazing house. Before the car had come to a halt, men in immaculate white livery and maroon caps leapt from both back doors. They were holding fire extinguishers that were significantly larger than the two used by Ludo and Sid.

The driver's door opened and out stepped a recognizable figure in a dark jacket and gray cap. It was none other than the Maharajah himself. Sid and Ludo rushed over to where he was opening the trunk of the car and pulled out two more large extinguishers. Brandishing the new tank, Ludo led the Maharajah's staff into the neighbor's house, while Sid and the Maharajah went into Ludo's. Two students grabbed the remaining extinguishers and followed them inside.

In less than a minute, all that remained of the fire were streams of dark, foamy liquid pouring down the sides of both houses and into the street, and the acrid smell of smoke and chemical fumes. In the distance we could hear a siren as the fire engine drew closer.

After the Maharajah and his two attendants left, the fire department surveyed the damage. Several support posts had been badly burned, and until they were replaced the balcony would be unsafe. The furniture had slid to one side, where the floor looked as if it might give way at any moment. Looking around the building that had been both his home and yoga studio for several decades, Ludo seemed relieved that it hadn't been completely destroyed. Despite the damage, he said things could have been much, much worse.

"If it hadn't been for the Maharajah," observed Serena, adjusting her favorite scarf around her shoulders, "who knows how things could have ended?"

There were murmurs of assent. Ludo and Sid exchanged a meaningful glance.

The students filtered back into the building, gathering as on evenings past, but on this occasion inside. Serena had ordered takeaway from the Himalaya Book Café, and large cardboard boxes of pizza were being passed around, along with a nerve-steadying carafe of red wine.

"What I'm trying to work out," mused Sukie, "is how the Maharajah knew about the fire."

"Perhaps someone phoned him," suggested Ewing.

"He's said to be very community minded," someone added.

"I've heard that, too," agreed Serena. "And he often seems to walk down this street in the evening. Maybe he saw the fire himself."

"Whatever the case, I'm not sure how I can possibly thank him for saving my house," said Ludo.

"He didn't want to stay for a glass of wine?" asked Merrilee in her smoker's voice, refreshing her own glass.

"He probably doesn't drink," said Sid. "And he's very private. Doesn't like a fuss."

"I'll have to arrange a personal meeting to thank him," proposed Ludo.

"Much better," agreed Sid. "But I think you are forgetting the *real* hero of the evening, without whom the fire would have done so much more damage before anyone even knew what was happening."

There was a pause before they all turned to look at me.

"Swami!"

"You are right," Ludo said, rising from his chair and coming over to where I was sitting next to Serena. He seemed to prostrate as he knelt on the rug in front of me.

"I don't think I will ever forget the sound you made," he said, stroking me appreciatively.

"Spine-chilling," remarked Merrilee with a shudder.

"Gave me goose bumps," said Sukie.

"You wonder how they know," mused Carlos, adjusting his trademark bandanna.

"Oh, I think cats know more than we give them credit for," said Ludo. "A lot more than we even recognize ourselves."

It was a moment before Serena said, "As we were discussing at the café earlier."

Ludo, Sid, and several others nodded in agreement.

For the benefit of those who hadn't been at lunch, Serena repeated what the eminent biologist had said about the consciousness of animals. "He told us that animals have the ability to perceive certain things imperceptible to humans."

Apparently, we are sentient in ways that most people never for a moment stop to consider.

"I once heard about a pet pig," said Ewing, "who woke up his owners by pulling off their bedcovers one night. The house was on fire, and they were sleeping through it. They reckon the pig saved their lives."

"Just like Swami helped save the studio and my home," observed Ludo.

"Do you think it was the scent of the fire she noticed?" asked a yogi called Jordan.

"Scent?"

"Or she could have seen smoke," suggested someone.

"Sixth sense," said Carlos, offering a more flattering explanation.

I remembered the huge rat that had appeared from nowhere and my shock at seeing it, followed by the involuntary yowl its appearance had provoked.

"She certainly knew how to warn us!" said Merrilee.

Ludo looked at me with an expression of profound gratitude. "For that, Swami will always be a guest of honor at our studio."

It was only later, as we were leaving and people were in the hallway putting on their shoes, that Merrilee noticed Serena's scarf.

"You were lucky," she said, taking the edge of it between her thumb and forefinger. "You normally leave this—"

"—on the balcony," Serena finished. "It would have gone up in smoke."

"But not tonight?"

"That's the weird thing," Serena said. "I could have sworn I put it outside. But apparently it was here, beside my bag, all along."

"You don't think . . . ?" Merrilee started to say.

"Here she is!" interjected Sid, stroking my face with his smooth fingertips as Serena held onto me. "A very special being."

What was it that made me feel so close to this tall Indian man with the sparkling eyes? "The one," he continued, "who knows much but says little."

I looked up at Sid, recollecting the rat on the scarf. If *I* knew much but said little, what could be said of him?

Later that evening I curled up on the yak blanket that His Holiness kept on his bed for my exclusive use. As I hovered in that gentle, drowsy state between wakefulness and sleep, images from last night's dream and this evening's fire flashed through my mind, and I thought about what the biologist had said about the sentience of animals. It occurred to me that one of the most obvious but overlooked facts about happiness is that all of us *sem chens*—humans, felines, even rats—are equal in our wish to attain it. If each of us has been some other kind of *sem chen* in a previous life, and might be again in the future, then the happiness of all living beings, whatever the species, is our only worthy goal.

Chapter Eight

Exploring the art of purring had taken more intriguing twists than I could ever have imagined. But despite the wisdom I had gained in the past few weeks, there was still, dear reader, a very basic question about happiness that troubled me: why could I be contentedly padding along, minding my own business, when for no reason at all a sense of disgruntlement would come over me? A productive morning of meditation, grooming, and cello-recital—as we cats refer to that most intimate part of our grooming routine—could inexplicably turn bleak and gray. An afternoon down at the Himalaya Book Café that began with the wonderfully promising arrival of a plate of poached sea trout could draw to a sluggish and querulous close. Nothing in particular might have happened to cause this change of feeling. Had I been shooed off a windowsill, had my tail tugged by a spiteful child, or been prodded from a catnap for an enforced photo opportunity—such is the price of fame—my peevishness would be perfectly understandable.

But I hadn't. So it isn't.

The wisdom I'd received sitting on the lap of the Dalai Lama had made me much more aware of what went on in my mind and much less prone to these invisible ups and downs. Even so, there could be no denying that warm, good feelings could subtly give way to a darker mood. And so it was when one morning, without any effort on my part, the truth was revealed in all its perfect obviousness.

It started when Tenzin came over to where I was sprawled across the top of the filing cabinet.

"You may be interested to know, HHC, that your favorite person in the world is coming in this morning."

The Dalai Lama? By my reckoning he was exactly nine sleeps away, not counting catnaps.

"In a couple of weeks, His Holiness will be back among us," Tenzin continued. "From the moment he gets back he has a *very* busy schedule. Lots of guests to cater for. Which is why our VIP chef is coming to take stock. She wants everything shipshape ahead of his arrival."

Mrs. Trinci was coming! The queen of Jokhang's kitchen and my generous benefactor!

As Tenzin stroked my cheek I seized his forefinger between my teeth, holding it for a few moments before licking away the trace of carbolic.

Tenzin chuckled. "Oh, little Snow Lion, you're too funny. But Mrs. Trinci isn't cooking anything today, so don't go to the kitchen expecting any treats."

I met his cautionary expression with my most imperious blue gaze. For a seasoned diplomat, Tenzin could be remarkably obtuse. Did he seriously think that Mrs. Trinci could resist me, especially after such a long absence? A single look of blue-eyed tenderness was all it would take. Perhaps a beseeching curl of the tail around her leg. At the very most, a pleading meow, and Jokhang's VIP chef would be warming up a treat for my delectation faster than you could say "diced chicken liver."

With a spring in my admittedly erratic step, I was soon on my way downstairs.

I arrived in the kitchen to find Mrs. Trinci in her familiar apron, holding a clipboard and pen, calling out a list of items while Lobsang and Serena replied from the refrigeration room and pantry, respectively.

"Ten pints of natural Greek yogurt?"

"Yes," answered Lobsang.

"When do they expire?"

"End of next month."

"All of them?"

There was a pause.

"Yes."

"Pitted prunes? There should be four large tins."

"Only three," responded Serena.

"*Oh, porca miseria!*—bloody hell! Now I remember. One of the tins rusted through. We had to throw it out."

Seeing some movement out the corner of her eye, she turned to see me wobbling toward her.

"*Dolce Mio!*" In an instant her tone changed to such effusive adoration that even I found it hard to believe I was the cause of it.

"How is my little *bella,* my little beauty?" She swept me off my paws, showered me with kisses, and placed me on a counter. "I have missed you so much! Have you missed me?"

As she ran her bejeweled fingers through my thick coat, I purred appreciatively. This was a wonderfully familiar prelude to what was sure to be an even more delightfully rewarding experience.

"Are we finished in here?" Lobsang called out from the walk-in refrigerator.

"For the moment," Mrs. Trinci replied distractedly. "Tea break!"

Swooping into her tote bag, she took out a sealed plastic bowl and removed the lid. "I kept the tiniest soupçon of last night's goulash for you," she told me. "I warmed it up before coming. I hope it meets the standards of your rarefied palate."

Mrs. Trinci's Hungarian goulash was as deliciously succulent and its gravy as whisker-tinglingly sublime as any food could be.

"Oh, *tesorino,* my little treasure!" she exclaimed, studying me closely through her mascara-lashed amber eyes as I bent to devour the goulash with noisy delight. "You are truly," she pronounced breathlessly, "the Most Beautiful Creature That Ever Lived."

A short while later, Mrs. Trinci, Serena, and Lobsang were sitting on stools at the kitchen counter, sipping mugs of tea and munching on coconut slice that Mrs. Trinci had brought with her.

"Thank you, Mrs. Trinci," Lobsang said, holding up the piece he was eating and smiling broadly. "Very good of you to remember." Her coconut slice had been a favorite of his since childhood.

They all chuckled.

"Just like old times," said Serena.

"Ah, yes." Mrs. Trinci sighed happily. "When was the last time the three of us worked together here—twelve years ago?"

After a pause, Lobsang said, "I think fourteen."

"Who would have thought that my two kitchen hands would do so well for themselves, eh? The Dalai Lama's translator. A high-flying chef from Europe. Everything changes."

"Impermanence," agreed Lobsang.

"Well, not *everything* has changed," said Serena. "We're all a bit older; we've seen a bit of the world. But we're still the same people. Especially the way we feel about important things." She gazed at Lobsang. "That hasn't changed."

Lobsang stared into mid space contemplatively for a few moments before replying. "True. I still think your mother's coconut slice is the best of all confectionary."

As they laughed, he met Serena's eyes with a twinkle. "For example."

"For example," she repeated.

"I suppose that's why it's so difficult"—his expression suddenly became serious—"to change direction once you have set yourself on a particular course." The aura of tranquility that usually emanated from Lobsang had been replaced by uncertainty.

Mrs. Trinci gave Serena a meaningful glance. The two of them had evidently discussed whatever Lobsang was referring to. Unable to bear the change that had come over him, Mrs. Trinci got off her seat, walked over to him, and with a clash of bracelets, put her arms around him.

"Of course, this is a difficult time for you, my dear Lobsang," she said. "But you must know that whatever decision you come to, you will have my full support!"

Only a short while later, there was a polite knock on the kitchen door, then Lama Tsering stepped inside. Tall, thin, and with the most ascetic of faces, Lama Tsering was the disciplinarian of Namgyal Monastery—the one responsible for overseeing the behavior of the monks at temple services and as they were engaged in other practices. As soon as he appeared, Lobsang got off his stool, put down his mug, and brought his palms together at his heart.

Lama Tsering bowed deeply. "Good morning to you."

"Good morning, Lama." Mrs. Trinci seemed flustered by his presence.

"Tenzin told me you were here today," he said, meeting her eyes with an earnest expression. "I have come to ask, most sincerely, for your advice."

"*My* advice?" Mrs. Trinci squeaked, smiling nervously.

"On matters of nutrition," he continued.

"*Mama Mia!* I thought I had done something wrong!"

Lama Tsering tilted his head and with the tiniest hint of humor about his mouth said, "Why would you think that?"

Mrs. Trinci shook her head vigorously before passing him the tray of coconut slice. "Have a piece," she offered. "Cup of tea?"

Lama Tsering studied the tray with interest. "It looks very nice," he observed. "But first I need to know something." Retrieving a small notebook from the pocket of his robe, he flicked it open to a page on which he had taken notes. "Is this"—he consulted his writing—"low Glycemic Index? Low GI?"

"Pretty low," she assured him.

"Mum!" Serena rebuked her as Lama Tsering helped himself to a piece.

Mrs. Trinci shrugged. "Everything's relative."

Lama Tsering took an appreciative bite before observing, "Perhaps moderately low, then?"

"To extremely high," suggested Serena, before all of them, even Lama Tsering, burst out laughing.

"Why the interest in GI?" Mrs. Trinci asked the lama after a moment.

"As disciplinarian at the monastery," he replied, "it is my duty to ensure that all the monks are practicing well, are exercising self-control, and, above all, are content." He patted his heart. "But I have only recently discovered how important nutrition is to this."

"A balanced diet," offered Serena.

"Glucose, in particular," Lama Tsering said with such authority that it was evident he had done his homework—just as it was evident to Lama Tsering that we had never given one moment's thought to the subject.

"Our monks need two things to enjoy fulfillment and success: intelligence and self-control. Of these two, there is no known method to increase intelligence. But self-control—willpower—this is something different. Even in the West, scientists are discovering the importance of emotional intelligence."

Lobsang nodded. He was very well acquainted with the work of Daniel Goleman, who had spent much time with His Holiness and whose books on emotional intelligence and social intelligence were known worldwide.

"The marshmallow experiment at Stanford University," Lobsang said.

"A highly effective predictor of success," confirmed

Lama Tsering. Then glancing at the looks of puzzlement on the faces of Mrs. Trinci and Serena, he went on. "In the 1960s, young children were shown into a room, one at a time, and researchers made a deal with them. Each child was given a marshmallow and told that they could eat it right away if they liked, but if they waited for the researchers to return after stepping out for a bit, they could have an additional marshmallow. The researchers left the room for fifteen minutes. Some children ate the sweet immediately. Others were able to restrain themselves and ended up with two marshmallows.

"Those children who had more self-control when they were young went on to achieve higher grades, have fewer problems with drink or drugs, and earn more money. Scientists are showing that self-control is a better indicator of future success than even intelligence."

"Oh dear," murmured Mrs. Trinci. "I would have eaten the marshmallow straight away!"

Lama Tsering ignored the interjection. "The same thing has been observed over many years with our monks. It is not always the most intelligent who attain realization. It is those who are willing to apply themselves."

"But how does glucose affect this?" asked Serena.

"I have learned recently that one of the main factors affecting willpower is how much glucose we have in our system," Lama Tsering said. "Low levels of glucose lead to less self-regulation, less ability to control thoughts, emotions, impulses, and behavior. When it is a long time since they have eaten, most people feel stressed and can't think as clearly."

"Yes, I've heard something about this," Lobsang said, animated by a recollection. "A study about whether or not prisoners would be granted parole."

Mrs. Trinci and Serena looked at him with interest. "In the end," Lobsang told them, "it had nothing to do with what crime the prisoners had committed, or their behavior in jail, or their race, or any other variable you might suspect. It had to do with the time of day they appeared before the parole board and how tired or hungry the board members were. The sooner it was after breakfast or lunch, the more likely prisoners were to be granted parole. But as the morning or afternoon wore on, members of the parole board grew increasingly tired and hungry and were more likely to deny parole."

"That's a very good example," Lama Tsering said, making a note of it. "And I think we have all experienced this. When we are tired and hungry everything becomes a big effort."

"Which is exactly why we are enjoying our coconut slice," chimed in Mrs. Trinci. "And why I always make sure His Holiness's little Snow Lion never suffers from . . ." She trailed off, searching for the right term.

"Decision-fatigue?" suggested Lobsang.

As long as my belly was full of goulash, he could make as many jokes at my expense as he liked, I thought, licking the last vestiges of rich gravy from the bowl.

"So, Mrs. Trinci," Lama Tsering said, waving a sheaf of papers in his right hand. "I have with me here the official menu from the monastery kitchens. I wonder if you can advise how it might be improved."

"To make the meals lower GI?" she asked.

"Exactly."

"You need to go for the slow burn," she said, reaching for the papers. "Nuts, vegetables, raw fruits, cheese, oils, and other good fats. Foods that lead to better blood sugar balance." Scanning the list, she started shaking her head. "White rice? White bread? Every day? Oh, no, this is too much!"

Lama Tsering watched her scrutinize the list with an approving air. "It will be interesting," he said, "to observe what a difference a few simple changes in the kitchen may make."

As it happened, new menu items were also being keenly discussed at the Himalaya Book Café. In particular, an intriguing new opportunity had presented itself since Serena's inaugural Indian banquet.

As the date of the second banquet drew closer, there was a steady stream of bookings from local residents who had attended the first one and friends who had heard their rave reviews, as well as hotel managers whose visitors could be guaranteed a memorable night out. Without the need for so much as a poster in the window, a week before the second Indian banquet, the café was fully booked.

What's more, some of those who had come to the first banquet had asked Serena, as a special favor, for the recipe for their favorite dish. For some it had been vegetable *pakoras*. For others the Malabar fish curry. Ever generous, Serena had obliged, happily giving them the recipes that she and the Dragpa brothers had spent so much time refining, adjusting, and perfecting.

But to no avail.

It was Helen Cartwright, Serena's friend from school days, who was the first to complain. She and Serena were having a mid-morning cappuccino about a week after

Serena had given her the mango chicken recipe. From the magazine rack I overheard Helen saying she had set about preparing it as a special treat for the family, only to end up with a bland imitation of Serena's gastronomic triumph.

Had she followed every step of the instructions? a puzzled Serena wanted to know. Had the chicken been left to marinate? And for how long? It was only after quite some discussion that Serena identified the real reason for Helen's disappointment.

That conversation was followed by a similar one just a few days later. Merrilee from yoga class had attempted Serena's *rogan josh* recipe with equally lackluster results. On this occasion, Serena had gone straight to the heart of the matter. Had Merrilee included all the spices on the list? We-e-ell, most of them, Merrilee told her. In some cases, where she didn't have the right spice—there were so many of them, after all—Merrilee had tried a substitute. How fresh were the spices? demanded Serena. Merrilee had been forced to confess that at least one of the seasonings had been sitting at the back of her spice rack for nearly ten years. Maybe more.

After Serena pointed out the obvious reason for her culinary flop, Merrilee looked abashed for a moment before she proposed—only half-jokingly—that if Serena would provide her not just with the recipe but also with the correct blend of fresh spices, then she would be assured success in the kitchen.

A less compassionate person might have dismissed this request without a second thought. But reflecting on her friends' disappointment and the unlikelihood they would ever have easy access to the array of fresh, quality spices she kept in the storeroom, Serena decided to oblige. At her request, the Dragpa brothers made up sealed sachets of blended spices for the mango chicken and *rogan josh* recipes. Serena gave one of each to Helen and Merrilee.

She didn't have long to wait for their response. Within days they had returned, ecstatic over the deliciousness of their meals and the rave reviews of family and friends. Both of them also confessed to feeling unworthy of the praise. Helen summed it up: "I didn't actually *do* anything. Anyone can sprinkle stuff on a piece of chicken and then grill it half an hour later. It's the spices that make the dish."

It was Merrilee who suggested a commercial angle. "Why don't you put the blended spices on sale?" she proposed. "I'd be your first customer."

Serena had taken her suggestion, combining the spice sachet with rice and nuts so that the only things left to buy were fresh vegetables or meat. Using his computer, Sam designed and printed up the recipe on amber-colored paper under the Himalaya Book Café logo.

Spice packs were soon flying out the door to Serena's circle of friends, as well as to café regulars and students from the yoga studio. Once word got out, the small display box on the counter was soon replaced by a bigger box. And the day after Sam sent out a notice about the spice packs to everyone who had attended the first Indian banquet, orders came in for ten times the quantities made so far. There were even requests from as far afield as Seoul, Krakow, Miami, and Prague, from travelers who had dined at the café while visiting Dharamsala. People were very willing to pay for the convenience of being able to make an amazing meal with minimal thought or preparation time.

After the initial flurry of excitement, interest in the spice packs showed no signs of abating. The delicious results they delivered almost guaranteed that as soon as people used one pack they would want to order another. Perhaps several. In every flavor. Far from being a one-off or a fad, the spice packs grew in popularity as each week brought new customers through the door of the café and reorders online.

It was over an end-of-the-day hot chocolate that Sam made his extraordinary revelation. "How is it going with Bhadrak?" he asked Serena. A teenage nephew of the chefs, Bhadrak had been hired part-time for the sole purpose of making up spice sachets under the watchful eyes of his uncles, when the task had grown too big for them.

"Seems to be working out well," Serena said. "He's slow, very slow, but meticulous. I'd rather have that than the other."

"Quality control," agreed Sam.

"His uncles have put the fear of God into him on that score," said Serena.

"Which particular god?" Sam asked.

"All of them!" she said, chuckling. Despite having been brought up in India, Serena still found the variety of deities quite bewildering.

"I was having some fun with a spreadsheet . . ." Sam nodded to some papers on the table between them.

"*Such* a Sam line, that!"

"Really, I think even *you* will find this interesting," he protested. "Over the past week I discovered a new trend in the spice packs. In retrospect, I suppose it was predictable, but I didn't see it coming."

Serena raised her eyebrows.

"Referred customers. And I'm not just talking local residents. We've been taking orders from friends of people who've visited the café. In one case, a delicatessen in Portland, Oregon, ordered twenty packs of every kind."

"Bhadrak *will* be kept busy," said Serena.

Sam realized that Serena still wasn't seeing what was so apparent to him. "I think it could go beyond that. All this interest after just one Indian banquet and with no online promotion. We don't even have spice packs among the items listed on our website."

"Probably just a flash in the pan," said Serena, shrugging. "In a couple of months the novelty will wear off and . . ."

"Or it could go the other way." The new, bolder Sam had no trouble voicing a counterargument. "The second banquet could build on the momentum of the first. You could include a spice pack for each diner, first one free. Even more people would try and buy." Picking up the papers on the table, he pulled out a page of projections and handed it to Serena.

"Look what happens if sales follow the same pattern as after the first banquet."

"What's this on the left?" Serena asked, pointing to one of the graphs.

"Sales in US dollars."

Serena looked surprised. "And the red?" She indicated a line that angled upward sharply.

"That's based on a conservative projection of what will happen if we promote the spice packs to everyone on the database."

"Amazing!" Serena's eyes widened.

"I haven't even factored in anything else that may happen. Like if you were to get some publicity. Online promotion. Perhaps repeat orders from that deli in Portland or others like it."

Serena sat up straighter on the sofa. "These figures . . ." She was shaking her head in amazement.

"*Now* can you see why I said it was fun?" he joked.

She nodded, flashing a smile.

"More than just fun," Sam amended. "The great thing about this is that it gets us into repeat business. Tourists will visit the café two or three times at most. They may buy a couple of books or gifts, and they're done. But what you've created gives them the opportunity to, quite literally, keep tasting their holiday again and again."

"Keeps the relationship going," added Serena.

"Exactly!" Sam's eyes were gleaming. "And more than that, look at the numbers."

"I can see. With that kind of volume we'd need a lot more than a part-time Bhadrak and some visits to the market. I'd need to find a source to guarantee our spice supply."

"Problems worth solving," said Sam, urging her to flip to the final page, which showed revenues for the café and bookstore, plus projected revenue for the spice packs. "Just check out the bottom line."

"Wow!" She stared at the figures.

After a pause, he told her, "It's a whole new business, Serena."

For a long while they both studied the figures, Serena aglow with the possibilities. Then her expression turned serious. "Have you heard from Franc about the accounts?" she asked.

The question held more significance than it seemed. Because of all that Franc was going through around his father's death, Serena and Sam had decided not to make a big deal out of the first Indian banquet. But they had shown it as a separate line item in the accounts they sent Franc each month, along with a brief explanation of each item. The separate line for the banquet showed a record high take on a night when the café was usually shut. And they had asked him, "Do you like?"

Seeing her expression, Sam shook his head no.

"Until we hear . . ."

Sam gathered the papers and put them in a pile on the coffee table. "I guess," he said.

For a while the two of them sat stroking their *sem chen* friends, the two dogs grinding their heads into the cushions with pleasure, while I signaled my contentment with a more genteel purr.

"Speaking of food," mused Serena after a while, "I heard some interesting things today about nutrition and self-control." She described the visit from the disciplinarian of Namgyal Monastery.

"I wonder if it's the same for these little ones," she said, looking at the dogs and me. "I'm guessing that nutrition may have an effect on how they're feeling at any particular moment of the day."

Sam glanced up momentarily, searching through his encyclopedic memory. "I remember reading somewhere that the ideal diet for an adult cat is about fourteen mice-size portions a day."

"Fourteen?!" exclaimed Serena.

Sam shrugged. "Once you get rid of the fur and bone, the average mouse isn't very caloric."

"I guess not," Serena conceded.

"There probably are parallels with human nutrition. All animals need the right balance of water, protein, and vitamins."

"Amazing to think how much our moods are affected by the food we eat," mused Serena.

"Happiness is chemistry," said Sam.

Serena looked dubious. "Maybe not exclusively. But the chemistry has to be there."

"A factor."

"An *important* factor," she amended.

"Oh, little Rinpoche," she said, leaning over and kissing my head effusively. "I so hope you're a chemically content little Snow Lion!"

Yes, I thought. After a mouse-size portion of lactose-free milk, I most certainly was. And along with the tasty meals I had eaten today—Mrs. Trinci's delicious goulash being the unquestioned highlight—I had also come to a surprising insight about happiness, one that might otherwise have remained a deep mystery.

I had discovered the reason why on a perfectly delightful morning I could suddenly feel testy and bored. The reason, dear reader, is *food*. For humans, a low-glucose diet appears to be the best way to ward off feelings of ennui and disgruntlement, and the possibility of denying parole-seekers their liberty. As for us felines, what could set the world right more reliably than a tasty mouse-size snack?

It was two days later when Sam summoned Serena over from the café area.

As she approached she saw him sitting grim-faced at his computer. "Just heard from Franc about the accounts," he told her.

She didn't need to look at the screen to guess the outcome. But when she did, she saw Franc's response to their question *Do you like?* At the bottom of the page, in large capitals he had written, "I DON'T LIKE!" He had even underlined the words for added emphasis.

Sam was shaking his head. "I just don't get it."

"I'm not completely surprised," said Serena, stepping back from the computer. "Franc's vision for the café has always been a Western oasis, an enclave removed from the world outside."

"Even when our customers are voting big-time with their wallets?"

Serena shrugged, but there was no mistaking the disappointment on her face. All thought of future Indian banquets, spice packs, and online promotions vanished in an instant. And with it came a sense of foreboding about what lay ahead for the Himalaya Book Café: we were heading into uncharted waters.

Chapter Nine

There can be few things more disagreeable than discovering a man with a face like a monkey parked in the seat of a much-loved friend.

Well, perhaps there are one or two things more disagreeable, such as being chased up a high wall by a pair of slavering retrievers or discovering that you were a dog in a previous life. Still, you can understand my dismay the morning I sidled into the executive assistants' office, roughly a week before the Dalai Lama was due home, and instead of finding the desk chair opposite Tenzin empty, it was occupied by a small, gnarled monk. I was so shocked when I saw his wizened face that I almost fell over backward. He had a tiny mouth, buckteeth, and no chin at all. His expression seemed fixed in a grimace.

I asked myself if this was actually happening, or if I was having one of those crazy, fitful, predawn dreams. But no, everything else was just as it should be. Tenzin was calmly writing a letter to the president of France.

From across the courtyard came the sound of chanting monks. The scent of roast coffee intermingled with Nag Champa incense was wafting down the corridor. It was just another day at the office—except for this strange apparition.

Tenzin greeted me with his usual formality. "Good morning, HHC."

I took a few steps in his direction and then glanced over my shoulder.

"The Dalai Lama's Cat," he explained to the other man. "She likes sitting on our filing cabinet."

The monk grunted in acknowledgment, flashing only the briefest of looks in my direction, before continuing to work at Chogyal's computer.

I am, dear reader, used to many different reactions to my appearance, from being pursued by the hounds of the hell realms to being prostrated before by the Namgyal monks. What I am *not* accustomed to is being ignored. Crouching for a moment, I launched myself into the air, landing with an unsteady thud on Chogyal's desk. *Well,* I thought, *Venerable Monkey Face can't ignore me now.*

But he did! There was an initial moment of disbelief as he stared at my sumptuously fluffy and—to most people—irresistible form perched on an ancient text. Then he abruptly turned back to his computer screen as if by pretending this wasn't actually happening, he could make it go away.

I was getting far more attention from Tenzin, who was following my movements with his usual diplomatic inscrutability. But I knew him well enough to realize that a lot was going on behind that poker face. If I wasn't mistaken, he seemed to find my unscheduled appearance quite amusing.

After long minutes during which the monk continued to ignore me, his eyes glued to the screen as though his life depended on it, I realized there was nothing to be gained by sitting on his desk. Instead, I ambled over to Tenzin's desk, taking care to leave a paw mark on the elegant engraved stationery from the Élysée Palace that was lying there before sweeping my bushy tail across his wrist. That was my way of saying, "Come, come, dear Tenzin, you know and I know that something here isn't as it should be." Then I hopped up on the filing cabinet behind him and after the most cursory wash behind the ears, settled down for my morning nap.

But sleep wouldn't come. As I sat sphinxlike, paws tucked neatly beneath me, and gazed across the room, my thoughts returned to Monkey Face. It looked like he was working on something under Tenzin's supervision. But for how long? Would he be gone by the end of the morning? The day?

That was when a new thought alarmed me: What if he had been brought in do Chogyal's job? Could he be a full-time appointment? The very idea was a horror! There he sat, a little brooding cloud of intensity—nothing like the warm-hearted, roly-poly, and benevolent Chogyal. If Venerable Monkey Face was to be a permanent fixture, the executive assistants' office was not a place I would want to spend my time. From a welcoming sanctuary, conveniently close to the suite I shared with His Holiness, it would become a forbidding place to be studiously avoided. What a terrible turn of events! Where would I spend my time when the Dalai Lama was away? How could this be happening to me, HHC?

The monk was still there when I left for lunch at the Himalaya Book Café, but, thankfully, he was gone by the time I returned. I was pausing in the doorway, looking over to where Tenzin was busy filing some paperwork, when Lobsang arrived. After reaching down to stroke me several times, he stepped into the office, hands folded behind him, and leaned against the wall.

"So how did it go with the first on your short list?" he asked Tenzin, glancing toward where the monk had been sitting.

"He's very diligent. Razor-sharp intellect."

"Uh-huh."

"Gets through the work"—Tenzin snapped his fingers—"like that."

I was following the conversation closely, looking from one to the other.

"Highly regarded by the abbots of our major monasteries," said Lobsang.

Tenzin nodded. "Important."

"Critical."

There was a pause before Lobsang prompted, "I'm sensing a *but*."

Tenzin looked at him evenly. "If it was only the abbots he had to deal with, that would be one thing. But whoever takes the position has to get on with a wide variety of people." Glancing over at me, he quickly corrected himself—"beings."

Lobsang followed his glance. Unable to restrain himself, he came over, picked me up, and held me in his arms. "A bit lacking in his interpersonal skills, is he?"

"Very shy," said Tenzin. "He's fine talking about scriptural matters. There, he's on firm ground. But the biggest challenges of the role are always people problems. Conflict resolution."

"Giving people ladders to climb down."

"Exactly. Something Chogyal was very good at. He had a way of getting people to think that his ideas were their ideas and of appealing to their highest motives."

"A rare gift."

Tenzin nodded. "Tough act to follow."

Lobsang was massaging my forehead with his fingertips, just the way I liked it. "I take it he didn't warm to HHC?"

"Didn't seem to know how to react. It was like she'd arrived from outer space."

Lobsang chuckled. "So, what did he do?"

"He just ignored her."

"Ignored? How could he do such a thing to you?" Lobsang looked down into my big blue eyes. "Didn't he realize you have the final decision?"

"Exactly. Working out who *really* wields influence is another requirement of the job."

"And such beings are not always the ones you expect, are they, HHC?"

Two days later, I arrived to find Chogyal's chair occupied by a mountainous monk with a big, boulder-like head and the longest arms I'd ever seen.

"Oh, yes. And who is this?" Before you could say *Om mani padme hum* the monk had seized me by the scruff of the neck, lifted me up, and suspended me in midair, slowly strangling me as though I were some brazen intruder.

"That," explained Tenzin quickly, "is His Holiness's Cat. HHC. She likes sitting on our filing cabinet."

"I see." The giant stood up, grasped me with his

other hand, carried me over to the filing cabinet, and thumped me down on it so hard that pain jolted through my tender hindquarters.

"She's a beauty, isn't she?" he observed, crushing me as he ran his hand down my spine.

I meowed plaintively.

"She's very delicate," noted Tenzin. "And much loved."

As the monk returned to his seat, I shakily surveyed the office. Never before had I been treated so roughly in Jokhang. Never so casually grabbed by the neck and inspected like some zoological exhibit. For the first time I could remember, I actually felt afraid in this office. The monster didn't know his own strength. He hadn't meant to hurt me. In putting me on the filing cabinet, he probably thought he was saving me the effort of jumping up there myself. But now all I could think about was how to escape as quickly as possible from the office without him touching me again.

I sat there, anxiously awaiting my moment. While Tenzin worked through the recommendations of a Red Cross proposal, at the desk facing him the Cat Strangler was a whirlwind of activity. E-mails were drafted and documents read. Summary notes were stapled to them—all with great energy. Drawers were slammed shut. The telephone was smashed back in its cradle. The very air in the office jangled with activity, and at one point when Tenzin made a joke, the great monster laughed from his belly, great gusts of hilarity reverberating along the executive floor.

The moment he announced he was going to make himself a coffee and offered to make one for Tenzin, too, I slipped down from the filing cabinet and made my escape. As I hurried away to the Himalaya Book Café much earlier than usual, I found myself thinking how, by comparison, Venerable Monkey Face was infinitely preferable. My feelings had been hurt when he ignored me, but I had come to realize that it was his problem, not mine. On the other hand, the red-robed giant was a physical threat. If he were chosen as Chogyal's successor, much of my life at Jokhang would be spent trying to avoid him.

And what kind of life was that?

Jangled, I made my way into the comforting environs of the café. With the constant swell and ebb of diners and book buyers, there was always plenty of bustle, but I felt safe here. I had certainly never been rough-handled by a giant—red-robed or otherwise.

Only halfway up the magazine rack to my usual spot on the top shelf, I became aware that something unusual was going on in the corner of the bookstore where we often gathered for our end-of-the-day treats. Serena and Sam were standing close together, whispering in an urgent, confidential manner.

"Who s-s-says so?" Sam was asking.

"Helen Cartwright's friend knows his sister, Beryle, in San Francisco."

"And when?"

"Soon, very soon." Serena's eyes were wide. "Like, in the next two weeks."

Sam was shaking his head. "That can't be right."

"Why not?"

"He would have told us. E-mailed something."

"He's not obliged to." Serena bit her lip. "He can come back whenever he likes."

For a while they both looked at the floor. Finally, Serena said, "Kind of puts the spice-packs thing into perspective. Doesn't matter what Franc thinks if I'm not even working here."

"You d-d-don't know that." Sam's authority had deserted him.

"That was the deal. I'm just a caretaker. A stopgap. When we made the agreement, I was planning to go back to Europe."

"Why don't we phone him?"

She shook her head. "It's his right, Sam. His business. I guess this was always going to happen."

"Perhaps we can ask around. Could be just a rumor."

When their conversation concluded I continued to the top shelf and settled down in croissant pose. Although she hadn't been here for long, Serena had brought a warmth and vibrancy to the café that made it even more special. That she might have to leave was something I didn't want to contemplate, especially with all that was going on up the hill.

The next day I was at the café early again, having slipped out of Jokhang in case the Cat Strangler returned. When Serena arrived for the day, I could tell that the news wasn't good. She approached Sam, who was shelving a new delivery of books, and told him what had happened at yoga class the evening before. One of her fellow students, Reg Goel, who was one of McLeod Ganj's best-known property agents, was keeping an eye on Franc's house while he was away. As they were returning their bolsters, blankets, and wooden bricks after class, Serena had asked Reg if he had heard from Franc.

Oh yes, Reg had replied breezily. He had been at Franc's place that very morning to oversee the removal of dustcovers from the furniture, the return of house plants to their proper places, and the restocking of the pantry and fridge. Franc had called him last week. He was due back any day.

Serena had been so shocked that she had hardly known what to say. She hadn't felt in any mood to stay for the postyoga tea session. As it happened, Sid had been in the hallway at the same time, and seeing the expression on her face, he had asked her if anything was wrong.

To her embarrassment, she had started to cry. Sid had shielded her discreetly before anyone else could see and had walked her back to the café. She had explained to him that the arrangement with Franc had only ever been temporary and that his return would mean she would be out of a job.

Shortly after ten the next morning, who should arrive at the café but Sid. I didn't recognize him at first, having only seen him in his yoga clothes. As he stood in the doorway, tall and elegant in his dark suit, he emanated a certain poise that was almost regal.

Serena approached him, gesturing her surprise and delight at his appearance.

"Actually, I came to see you," Sid explained, leading her to the back of the restaurant and the banquette that Gordon Finlay had favored in times gone by. It was the perfect place for a private conversation.

"I'm sorry I made an idiot of myself last night," Serena told him, after they were seated and had ordered coffees from Kusali.

"Don't say that," Sid told her protectively. "Anyone in your position would have felt the same." He looked at her closely for a while, eyes filled with concern. "I've been giving some thought to your situation. If the worst were to happen and you found yourself without a job, you would still want to stay in McLeod Ganj, wouldn't you?"

She nodded. "But that may not be possible, Sid. I need a job—and not just any job. I used to think that working in one of Europe's top restaurants was all I ever wanted. But the longer I stay here, the more I realize that it wouldn't really fulfill me. I've discovered other things that reward me in more important ways."

"Like the curries and spice packs?"

She shrugged. "All a bit hypothetical now, isn't it?"

He leaned against the banquette. "Or is it?'"

Her forehead wrinkled.

"I remember you telling the yoga group how popular the spice packs had become," he said. "How you had to take on a new employee just to handle the orders."

"He's in there right now," she said, tilting her head in the direction of the kitchen. "An order for another two hundred came in overnight."

"My point exactly."

"But if I'm not working here . . ." She trailed off, not following him.

"You also said that Franc doesn't want to continue with the curries and so on."

She nodded.

"What I'm thinking," Sid said, "is that if he returns as manager and keeps to his usual menu, it wouldn't be a conflict of interest for you to continue manufacturing spice packs."

Her eyes widened. "But where?"

"There are many premises available around here."

"I don't know, Sid. As it is we're starting to run into supply problems."

"With the spices?"

"The Dharamsala markets are fine for medium-size quantities. But we need guaranteed continuity of the best-quality spices in larger amounts."

"That," Sid told her emphatically, "is something I can easily arrange."

"How?"

"Through my business. We have access to producers across the region."

"I thought you were in IT," she said, her bewilderment deepening.

He nodded. "Among other things. Issues like fair trade in organic spices—these are very important to our community and important to me."

During the postyoga conversations on Ludo's balcony, Sid often referred to *our community*. This was something, Serena began to realize, that stemmed from a deeply held personal concern. But his mention of *organic* rang alarm bells. "What about pricing?"

"We would be buying direct. The cost would probably be less than what you pay in the market."

He had said *we*, she noticed, sipping her coffee. She set down her cup and placed her hand on the table. "Even if I were to, you know, set up a separate business, the only reason spice packs have taken off is because of the Himalaya Book Café."

Sid smiled, his eyes glowing with affection. He reached out and briefly rested his hand on hers. "Serena, the Himalaya Book Café was the reason you came up with the idea. But a successful business model doesn't depend on it. The two are entirely separate."

As Serena looked at him, the truth of what he was saying dawned on her. Of course the reason why people kept reordering spice packs wasn't because of the Himalaya Book Café but rather because of taste, convenience, and price. But more important to her at this moment was the truth of *why* he was saying it. Sid had evidently given a great deal of thought to her and the challenges she faced—much more than she would have thought likely even a day ago.

As Serena considered this, other things were swiftly flashing through her mind. Like how often Sid sat next to her on the balcony after yoga class. How delighted he had been when she announced her intention to stay in McLeod Ganj instead of returning to Europe. How concerned he had been when she mentioned that Franc had lost his father. All of this was pointing in the same direction.

Just as Sam had remained oblivious to Bronnie until she was standing across the counter from him shaking his hand, for the first time Serena actually *noticed* Sid. He might have been there all along, but only now was she beginning to understand—and smiling at the realization.

"What about marketing?" she questioned, somewhat distracted. "The customer database belongs to the Himalaya Book Café."

"Franc seems to be a reasonable man," said Sid. "Even if *he* didn't want to continue the spice-pack business, there would be no conflict if he referred business to you, perhaps for a royalty."

She nodded. "That would be fine as supplementary income. But if I were to go out on my own . . ."

"You'd need much wider distribution, ideally over-seas. And there is someone who can probably help you."

"Oh?"

"You've already met him."

That line again. "Here?"

"I don't remember his name, but you mentioned that he was one of the most successful businessmen in the fast-food industry."

Gordon Finlay, thought Serena. "Wow!" she said aloud. "If he opened the door to just one retail chain . . ." She was shaking her head. "I can't believe I didn't think of him."

"Sometimes it's easier to see these things from afar."

For the longest time they held each other's gaze.

"This is . . . amazing!" Serena said eventually. This time it was she who reached across the table, taking his hand between hers. "Thank you, Sid, for everything."

He nodded deeply, smiling.

"Do you have a business card or something?" Serena asked. "In case we need to talk more?"

"You'll find me at yoga," he said.

"You're always so conscientious," she told him. "But I may not be there regularly this week."

"I won't be missing any classes."

There was a curious pause before she persisted. "If I could just have a phone number or something?"

After a moment, and perhaps with some reluctance, Sid reached into his jacket pocket, took out a black leather wallet, and retrieved a card.

"It doesn't have your name on it," observed Serena as he handed it to her. "Just an address and phone number."

"Ask for Sid."

"They'll know who you are?"

Sid chuckled. "Yes, they all know me."

Serena was distracted for the rest of the day. There were moments when I looked up to see her behind the counter staring into the mid distance—something I'd never seen her do before. On one occasion she carried a bottle of chilled Sauvignon Blanc from the wine cellar to the kitchen instead of to the customer's table. On another she waved good-bye to a customer without giving him his change. She was going through the motions of being maître d', but her thoughts were evidently elsewhere.

Sid's visit had been as much a shock as a joy. How could she have missed it? Her own feelings had been etched in the delight on her face as he had reached out to touch her. And she had been unusually self-conscious as she realized just how much careful thought he had devoted to her situation. But now that he was no longer there, her thoughts were clouded by doubt. The news of Franc's imminent return, the revelation of Sid's interest in her, his bold but scary business proposals—it was a lot to take in. Why did everything always have to happen at once?

Shortly after lunch, a succulent feast of tender sole meunière that I devoured gratefully, I heard her replaying some of Sid's suggestions to Sam, but veiled in reservations. "I'm not sure Franc *would* be willing to let me use the mailing list," she said, confiding her doubts. "Seems he doesn't want the café to have those associations."

Sam was silent.

"Even if Gordon Finlay *did* open doors for me," she continued, "it's a long way from that to a steady flow of retail orders. How would I pay the bills in the meantime?"

It was a strange afternoon. The Himalaya Book Café was usually such a convivial place to spend time, but today it was as though the familiar music of the café had been transposed into a minor key. Dark clouds rolled across the sky, and the breeze grew so chilly that by three o'clock, Kusali had to swing the glass doors shut.

For my own part, I remained only because I was so afraid of what I might encounter if I returned to Jokhang during working hours. The very idea of the giant monk setting finger on me sent a shudder through my fluffy, gray boots. Though His Holiness's arrival was only days away, the threat of the giant monk dampened my excitement.

For Serena, it seemed that whatever excitement she might be feeling after Sid's visit was more than tempered by her worries about Franc's imminent return.

And that evening's hot-chocolate session seemed to confirm how dangerously unsteady things had become. After the usual exchange of signals between Serena and Sam, she had made her way to their spot, followed soon afterward by Kusali. On his tray were three mugs of hot chocolate—Bronnie had also become a regular—along with the dog biscuits and my milk.

Marcel and Kyi Kyi were soon attacking their biscuits ravenously, as though it was the first food they had seen all day. I attended to my milk with somewhat more decorum. Sam came over from the bookstore and sat down heavily opposite Serena.

"Bronnie coming down?" Serena asked, nodded at the third mug of chocolate on the tray.

"Not this evening," Sam said wearily. Then, after a pause, "Maybe never."

"Oh, Sam!" Serena's face filled with concern.

He took a long sip of chocolate before glancing at her only briefly. "Big argument," he said.

"Lovers tiff?"

He was shaking his head sadly. "More."

Serena remained silent before he told her, "Says she's always wanted to go to K-K-Kathmandu. A volunteering job has come up there. She doesn't seem to understand that I can't just walk away from the bookstore to go with her."

Serena pursed her lips. "Difficult."

Sam sighed deeply. "The job or my girlfriend. Great choice."

There was no one in the bookstore by now, and only one table of diners remained in the café—four regulars idling over the remnants of their crème brûlée and coffee. With Kusali still on duty, neither Serena nor Sam was paying much attention to what was happening beyond their table, which was why they were caught completely off guard by the arrival of a visitor who seemed to materialize out of nowhere. As Franc's teacher and self-appointed adviser to Sam, he was no stranger to the café, but he hadn't been seen here in quite a while. This visitor only came here for a specific purpose.

Sensing a movement on the stairs to the bookstore, Sam looked up to see him standing at the end of their table. "Geshe Wangpo!" he exclaimed, wide-eyed.

Sam and Serena both started to get to their feet.

"Stay!" Geshe Wangpo commanded, palms facing toward them both. "I am here only for a short time, yes?" He perched on the armrest of Sam's sofa.

Geshe Wangpo was powerfully commanding, and his mere presence was enough to subdue everyone present into a state of meek compliance. As Serena made eye contact with Sam, Geshe Wangpo told them, "It is necessary to practice equanimity. When the mind is too much up and down there can be no happiness, no peace. This is not useful for self and"—he glanced pointedly at Serena—"not useful for others."

After Serena glanced down, I felt the force of Geshe Wangpo's gaze turn toward me, and it was as though I was an open book to him. He seemed to know exactly how I had felt about Venerable Monkey Face and the Cat Strangler. How I'd taken refuge in the café, frightened to return to Jokhang. How my usually boundless self-confidence had deserted me. As I gazed up at him, I sensed that he knew me as well as I knew myself.

Then Sam seemed to feel exposed and nodded ruefully. There could be no hiding from the self-evident truth.

After a moment, Serena spoke. "The problem is how."

"How?"

"It's so hard to stay level, to practice equanimity," Serena said, "when there's so much . . . stuff happening."

"Four tools," Geshe Wangpo said, looking at us each in turn. "First: impermanence. Never forget: *this, too, will pass.* The only thing you know for sure is that however things are now, they will change. If you feel bad now, no problem. Later you will feel better. You know this is true. It has always been true, correct? And it is still true now."

They were nodding.

"Second: what is the point of worrying? If you can do something about it, fix it. If not, what is the point of worrying about it? Let go! Every minute you spend worrying, you lose sixty seconds of happiness. Don't allow your thoughts to be like thieves, stealing your own contentment.

"Third: don't judge. When you say 'This is a bad thing that's happening,' how often are you wrong? Losing a job may be exactly what you need to start a more fulfilling career. The end of a relationship may open more possibilities than you even know exist. When it happens you think *bad*. Later you may think *the best thing that ever happened*. So don't judge, no matter how bad it seems at the time. You may be completely wrong."

Serena, Sam, and I stared at Geshe Wangpo, transfixed. In that moment he seemed like the Buddha himself, appearing directly in our midst to tell us exactly what we most needed to hear.

"Fourth: no swamp, no lotus. The most transcendent of flowers grows out of the filth of the swamp. Suffering is like the swamp. If it makes us more humble, more able to sympathize with others and more open to them, then we become capable of transformation and of becoming truly beautiful, like the lotus.

"Of course"—Geshe Wangpo rose from the armrest, having delivered his message—"I speak only of things on the surface of the ocean, the winds and storms that we all endure. But never forget"—he leaned across the table, touching his heart with his right hand—"deep down, under the surface, all is well. Mind is always pristine, boundless, radiant. The more you dwell in that place, the easier it will be to deal with temporary, surface things."

Geshe Wangpo was communicating with more than words. He was also showing us their meaning. In that moment the deep-down, all-is-well-ness of which he spoke had a palpable reality. Then he left, as noiselessly and unnoticed as when he had arrived.

For a while Serena and Sam sat back in the sofas, stunned by what had just happened.

Sam was the first to speak. "That was . . . pretty amazing. The way he just appeared."

Serena nodded with a smile.

"Seems he knows exactly what's going on in your mind," Sam continued.

"And not only when you're with him," Serena added.

Sam met her eyes for a long while, sharing her amazement.

"What he said was so right though," she said, smiling. She seemed to be acknowledging that a cloud had lifted.

Sam nodded. "Irritatingly so."

They both chuckled.

Kusali opened the front door, and an evening breeze rippled through the café. Over by the window, the last table of diners was preparing to leave.

I reflected on the significance of what Geshe Wangpo had said. Enduring happiness was only possible with equanimity. As long as our happiness depended on circumstances, it would be as fleeting and unreliable as the events themselves. Like wisps of discarded cat hair borne on the wind, our emotions would be tossed this way and that by forces quite beyond our control.

The tools for cultivating equanimity required no leap of faith. As Geshe Wangpo had explained them, they were self-evident. But at its heart, the essence of equanimity was familiarity with the nature of mind itself, something I knew must be developed through the practice of meditation. Geshe Wangpo had evidently mastered the practice. That much was apparent in the way the minds of others were so transparent to him—a natural consequence of his own mind being free of obscurations.

It was some time before Serena noticed. She looked quickly from Sam's face to the sofa, then beneath the table, then across to the basket under the counter.

"The dogs!" she exclaimed.

Sam sat up with a jolt, asking anxiously, "Where are they?"

Both of them stood and surveyed the café and bookstore.

And then Serena spotted them lying on the pavement, just outside the café door. Never in all our end-of-the-day sessions had Marcel and Kyi Kyi abandoned the sofa and the possibility of a tummy rub. Never had they gone out into the darkness at the end of the night. It just didn't happen.

Serena exchanged a look with Sam.

"They know," she said.

CHAPTER TEN

Indeed they did.

A short while later, Serena was tallying up the night's receipts, having waved goodnight to the last table of diners. Behind the bookstore counter, Sam was doing the same. Kusali was putting the finishing touches on the café in readiness for tomorrow's breakfast. Having made my way down from the book section, I was about to amble home.

There was a sudden commotion outside, and we all looked toward the door. A large, white taxi had pulled up beside the café, its lights ablaze. Someone was climbing out of the backseat. Marcel and Kyi Kyi were yapping crazily, jumping up at the figure in black jeans and a sweatshirt. Even before he turned, we knew exactly who it was.

He bent to take one dog in each arm. The barking abruptly stopped, replaced by a frenzy of snuffling, whimpering, and face licking. Franc threw back his head and laughed with joy.

When he stepped into the café, he looked from Serena to Sam to Kusali to me.

"I've come straight from Delhi. I made the cabdriver come past the café. When I saw the lights were on . . ." He didn't need to explain, as he clutched the two squirming dogs with delight.

Serena was the first to approach him. "Welcome home!" she said, planting a kiss on his cheek.

Franc put the dogs on the floor. They immediately hurtled up the steps as Sam was coming down, before racing back to Franc, then out the door onto the sidewalk, then back inside again.

"Great to have you back!" Sam greeted him with a handshake followed by a bear hug.

A short distance away, Kusali folded his palms at his heart and bowed deeply. Franc reciprocated, holding the headwaiter's gaze all the while. "*Namaste,* Kusali."

"*Namaste,* sir."

Then Franc came over to where I was sitting and took me in his arms. "Little Rinpoche," he said, kissing me on the neck. "I'm so glad you, too, are here. It wouldn't have been the same without you."

I snuggled into his arm.

Sam looked down at where the two dogs were still racing around in circles like crazy things. "I know I didn't say anything about returning," Franc told Sam and Serena. "That's because for the next little while I want you to carry on doing what you're doing."

"You think you could stay away from here?" Serena said with a smile, betraying none of the anxiety she was feeling.

"Oh, I'll be stopping by for coffee or lunch. But full-time manager?" He was shaking his head. "I'm not in any big hurry. One of the things that going through this whole experience with Dad made me realize is that I want to make the most of being here in McLeod Ganj with all these great teachers. Life is short. I don't want to spend all of it running a restaurant."

The three humans and I were listening intently.

"If you weren't going back to Europe"—he looked over at Serena—"I'd be trying to persuade you to stay on and job-share with me."

"*That's* an idea." Sam glanced over at Serena with a grin.

Serena raised her eyebrows. "You'd trust my judgment?"

Franc beamed. "Why wouldn't I? We've never had such great financials as we've had since the two of you began running the show. Everyone seems better off without me."

He cocked his head, looking at the dogs. "Hopefully not *everyone*."

Serena and Sam exchanged a meaningful glance.

"It's just . . ." began Serena at the same time that Sam said, "When we . . ."

Both stopped.

"What?" Franc looked from one to the other.

"The curry nights," Serena managed, only moments before Sam said, "Spice packs."

"Exactly!" Franc's eyes gleamed.

"But we thought . . ." began Serena.

"Your e-mail said . . ." continued Sam.

". . . that you didn't like the idea," Serena finished.

Franc frowned. "Last month's accounts?"

As they nodded, faces grave, he said, "I remember exactly what I wrote: *I DON'T LIKE. I LOVE!*"

Sam was suddenly besieged with emotion. "The bottom of the page must have been cut off!" He looked at Serena in abject apology. "We only got the first bit."

But Serena didn't care. Rapturous, she grabbed Franc and hugged him. "I can't tell you how happy that makes me!"

The next morning after breakfast, I emerged tentatively from the suite I shared with His Holiness and tiptoed down the corridor that led past the executive assistants' office. I was prepared to scamper back to my safe haven at the first sign of the Cat Strangler. Instead I heard Tenzin and Lobsang discussing some new development. Ever curious, I padded into the office.

". . . completely by surprise," Tenzin was saying, before catching sight of me.

They greeted me in chorus: "Good morning, HHC."

I made my way over and rubbed first against Lobsang's legs, then Tenzin's.

"The thing is, he gets back in three days and has a very busy schedule from the moment he returns," Tenzin said, resuming their conversation. He reached down for a moment to stroke me. "You hear that, HHC? In three days your favorite staff member will be bringing His Holiness back to us."

Although I arched my back in appreciation of his affection, the news that His Holiness's driver would be back at Jokhang thrilled me not one bit. I prided myself on being a cat of many names, but the name bestowed on me by this coarse fellow was shameful. It was one he had given me at the moment my very worst instincts had been provoked and I had brought a comatose mouse into Jokhang. Dear reader, can you believe what he named me, *me? Mousie Tung!*

"His Holiness knows what trouble we've been having finding someone for the job," said Tenzin. "With the ones we've short listed so far there has been a problem with skills or temperament, which is why he suggested this short-term solution."

I was greatly relieved. By the sounds of it, Chogyal's position was not going to be usurped by the Venerable Monkey Face. Nor would I have to flee past the executive assistants' office every day to escape the attention of the Cat Strangler.

"So when are you expecting your temp to arrive?" Lobsang asked.

Tenzin glanced at his watch. "Any minute. I just sent Tashi and Sashi to collect him."

Lobsang nodded. Glancing at the computer, he asked, "What about his IT skills?"

Tenzin shrugged. "I'm not sure he's even used a mobile phone before."

"On the other hand, being able to read people's minds certainly is an advantage," Lobsang observed.

They laughed before Tenzin said, "Some of His Holiness's decisions can seem strange at the time. But I have come to discover that very often, all is not as it seems."

A short while later Lobsang returned to his office, and I occupied my perch atop the filing cabinet. There was a flurry of small, bare feet on the corridor outside, accompanied by boyish voices. Then, without any detectable noise or movement, Yogi Tarchin appeared in the office. Just like the time I'd seen him at the Cartwrights', he was dressed in clothing that looked as though it came from a distant era, his robes a faded red brocade. There was a whiff of incense and cedar about him.

Tenzin rose to his feet. "Thank you so much for coming," he said, bowing deeply.

"It is my privilege to be able to serve His Holiness," Yogi Tarchin said, returning the bow. "My skills are few, but I am willing."

Tenzin gestured to the chair where Chogyal used to sit, before returning to his desk, so that they were facing each other.

"His Holiness holds you in the highest regard," Tenzin told Yogi Tarchin. "In particular he would greatly value your help with several sensitive monastic appointments he needs to make on his return."

I remembered how difficult Chogyal used to find these decisions. Monastic politics could be highly complex, and matters like scriptural authority, personality, and lineage had to be finely balanced.

But Yogi Tarchin merely chuckled. It was a laugh that instantly reminded me of someone else—His Holiness himself! It seemed to suggest that whatever the apparent gravity of a decision, when viewed from a perspective of abiding bliss and timelessness, it could be lightly worn.

"Oh, yes," said Yogi Tarchin. "When decisions are made for the good of all, they are easy. But if there is ego—quite difficult!"

Sitting opposite him, Tenzin seemed to be responding to the yogi's relaxed presence. I noticed him leaning farther back in his seat than usual, and his shoulders were less stiff.

"We do a fair amount of correspondence on the computer," Tenzin said, gesturing toward Chogyal's screen. "We can get someone to help you with the technical side."

"Very good," Yogi Tarchin said, swiveling the desk chair so he faced the screen, then grabbing the mouse and, with the ease of familiarity, flicking it about a few times. "Before my last retreat I used Microsoft Office. And who doesn't have an e-mail account? But no, apart from that, I'm not very computer literate."

Tenzin's expression was one of amazement. No doubt he was realizing that one should never be too quick to judge the capabilities of a yogi. After all, a mind that could penetrate the subtlest truths about the nature of reality was more than capable of creating a Word document.

As I adjusted my position on the filing cabinet, Yogi Tarchin looked up from his screen. "Oh—Little Sister!" he exclaimed, getting up from his chair and coming over to stroke me with great tenderness.

"That is His Holiness's Cat, otherwise known as HHC," explained Tenzin.

"I know. We have already met."

"Why *Little Sister?*"

"Just a name. She is my little Dharma sister," said Yogi Tarchin.

But both of us knew that he was making a reference to my relationship with Serena, the meaning of which was no clearer to me now than it had been when he had first said it. But it seemed, in that moment, that we now shared a secret, an understanding, the truth of which would be revealed in the fullness of time.

After Yogi Tarchin had returned to his desk, Tenzin glanced up at me and smiled. "I think you are friends," he observed.

Yogi Tarchin nodded. "For many lifetimes."

I noticed the difference the moment I stepped into the Himalaya Book Café: the basket under the counter was vacant. For the first time in my memory the café was canine free. I paused, more out of surprise than anything else. Strange though this confession may seem, for a moment I was actually quite disappointed. While Franc was away, the dogs and I had become good friends. But then I remembered Franc's surprise appearance the night before—how ecstatic the dogs had been to see him—and I was happy for them. No doubt they were back at home with Franc right now; all was well in their world.

That was how it felt inside the café, too. Last night's visit from Franc may have lasted only ten minutes, but it had the same effect as a breaking thunderstorm. All the tension that had been building during the previous days had been released in a single, cathartic moment. Serena was walking with a fresh spring in her step. Sam was bustling about, arranging a new, permanent display of spice packs. There even seemed to be a buzz among the waitstaff. No question, things were on an upswing at the Himalaya Book Café. And there was one person, more than any other, with whom Serena wanted to share the good news.

Several times I saw her approach the phone at the

reception counter, take out Sid's card, and lift the receiver. On each occasion something else came up demanding her immediate attention. With the constant activity, the front of the café wasn't exactly the best place to try to have a meaningful conversation. Which was when another thought seemed to occur to her.

Taking out Sid's card, she approached Kusali.

"Bougainvillea Street?" she queried. "That's the one that runs behind here, isn't it?" she asked. "The one I take up to yoga?"

"Yes, miss," he confirmed. Then as he looked at the card, Kusali said, "Number 108. That is the one with the high, white walls and metal gate."

"Really?" She glanced over in my direction. "I know the place. Some sort of business premises?"

He nodded. "I am thinking. There is always much coming and going from there."

I could see the direction her thoughts were taking, and my curiosity was instantly piqued. I remembered the rolling lawns and soaring cedars from the eternity I'd spent on top of the gatepost. I thought of the flower beds ablaze with color and fragrance, and the building that seemed to be substantial and rambling, with plenty of the nooks and crannies we cats so like to explore. I resolved to go visiting with Serena.

Remembering the length of the hill and the challenge of its gradient—would I ever forget?—I decided to get a head start. Leaving the café and following the lane behind it, all the while on retriever alert, I began my climb up Bougainvillea Street in the direction of the property with the high, white walls. I took care to stay close to the buildings, glancing behind me frequently, ready to run for cover if I saw either the retrievers or

Serena approaching. I knew that Serena wouldn't let me follow her so far from the café. But if I simply appeared as she was about to make her entrance, what choice would she have?

Which was why, when the pedestrian side gate was buzzed open after Serena announced herself on the intercom, I was there, quite casually, at her ankles. What a coincidence!

We went inside.

We followed a short, paved path to the house. There was a flight of marble steps to the front entrance, which was under a portico. With its columns and double French doors with polished brass hardware, the entryway had an air of formality.

Serena opened one of the doors, and we found ourselves in a large foyer with wood paneling, Indian carpets, and a long, very old-looking table that smelled of furniture polish. Otherwise, the room was empty. But it wasn't immediately apparent what sort of building we had stepped into. The entryway had neither the cold imper-sonality of an office foyer nor the welcoming warmth of a private home. Straight ahead was an open door leading into a corridor. To the left was another door that opened into a reception room. On the right was a flight of stairs.

While we were contemplating all this, a middle-aged man in a shirt and tie emerged from the corridor and walked toward us.

"May I help you, ma'am?" he asked, glancing with a somewhat startled expression at me sitting beside her.

Serena nodded. "Is Sid available, please?"

He looked bewildered.

"Sid," she repeated, seeking to dispel his confusion. "Perhaps he has something to do with IT?"

"IT?" he repeated, as if this was the first time he had heard the term. He shot a worried glance toward the stairs, before starting out in their direction.

"I will make a request," he said.

Before he had crossed the foyer, we heard a door opening somewhere above us, and then Sid appeared at the top of the stairs. Just as on the day before, he was wearing a dark suit and looking distinguished and important.

"I was glancing out the window a moment ago. I thought it was you," he said, sounding surprised. Pleased, too. But was there also a certain reserve?

"Thank you, Ajit," he said, dismissing the man who had greeted us.

Ajit bowed briefly before scurrying away.

As Sid descended the stairs, Serena glanced down at me and said, "I hope you don't mind, but it seems I was followed. I don't suppose you allow cats in here."

Reaching the bottom, Sid gestured with open arms. "Of course we do! Any time! An establishment that has no cat has no soul."

"I have some news I wanted to share with you in person," Serena told him. Her eyes were bright. "I hope it's all right coming to your office."

"Perfectly," he said, smiling. "Let's go somewhere where we won't be disturbed. I am, however, expecting a phone call any minute, which I will have to take."

He ushered us into a room with sofas, bay windows, and gilt-framed paintings, then continued through a set of glass doors to a veranda overlooking the lawns and gardens I had seen before, from a very different perspective. The veranda was furnished with comfortable cane furniture.

For a moment, Serena stood looking out, taking in the beauty of the grounds. There was a driveway hugging the perimeter of the property, shaded beneath tall pines. A flicker of movement through the trees caught her attention.

"Oh, look," she said, gesturing toward the white Mercedes moving toward up the driveway at a gracious speed. Behind the wheel was a distinctive figure in a dark jacket and gray cap. "Does he work from here?" Serena asked.

"He does," replied Sid, inviting her to sit.

"A drink?" he offered.

She shook her head. "I won't be long."

As he pulled up a chair opposite where she was sitting, I sniffed at the legs of the furniture, which had a tang of wax about them. Standing on my hind legs, I inspected the fabric on the cushions, worn with use. Even though I had never been here before, I felt immediately at home. I hopped up on the chair next to Serena's, so I could survey the scene around me.

"Franc made a surprise appearance at the café late last night," Serena began.

"So soon?"

She nodded. "He didn't give advance notice because he doesn't want to come back as manager. Not immediately. In fact"—a smile lit up her face—"he's talking about job sharing. He'd like more time outside the café."

"Really?" Sid sat forward in his chair.

"It gets better," Serena confided. "The whole thing about him not liking the curry nights and spice packs was a misunderstanding."

"What?"

"A classic," she said, shaking her head. "Turns out he wrote *I DON'T LIKE. I LOVE!* on the bottom of a page, but the scanner didn't pick up the last line."

Sid smiled, his features bright with possibility.

"So in one short visit . . . ?"

"Everything's different."

An urgent knocking on the glass door made them both look up.

A man in a shirt and tie looked at Sid imperatively, announcing, "Geneva is on the line."

"Sorry." Sid got up quickly. "I'll be as fast as I can."

Serena sat looking out at the gardens, enjoying the sunshine. Her gaze swept across the verdant foliage then returned to the door through which Sid had left. Curiosity getting the better of her, she made her way back into the reception room. Do I even need to say that I soon followed?

A massive fireplace with a mantle as high as Serena's shoulder dominated one wall. Above it hung a large, gilt-framed portrait of an Indian man wearing a turban, a Nehru-collared suit with jeweled buttons, and a sword at his waist. He had a stern expression—and an unmistakable familial resemblance to Sid.

A pair of curved, crossed swords sheathed in black leather and gold hung on another wall, alongside several silk banners embroidered with silver filigree. Serena took all this in before her attention was drawn to a highly polished occasional table with a cluster of framed family photographs on display. Some in sepia, others in full color, they showed generations of a family in single portraits and formal groups. There were several photographs of Sid with his parents, which she studied with close interest.

One side of the table was devoted to photographs of a young woman. In some she was with Sid, and in others they were accompanied by a little girl. There were also pictures of the girl alone as she grew older.

Near one of the bay windows there was a large painting of a palatial building with a golden dome. It was surrounded by high walls and sweeping palms—the kind of palace Serena had seen on the front of the glossy coffee-table books on Indian architecture that Sam sold in the bookstore. She stood looking at the painting for quite a while until the sound of voices outside caught her attention.

From the windows overlooking the driveway, we could see the white Mercedes, now parked under the portico. Standing beside it was the man in the dark jacket and gray cap—the one she had thought was the Maharajah. Addressing him was the man who had summoned Sid to the phone. While we couldn't hear details of the exchange between the two, it was clear that the one doing the talking was giving orders to the other man.

Serena watched them, deep in thought, trying to make sense of her enigmatic exchanges with Sid. "Someone said he's the Maharajah of Himachal Pradesh," she had told Sid that night returning from yoga. Sid had replied, "I've heard the same thing." He had been agreeing, she realized now, with what she had heard, not with whether it was true.

Then there was the unexplained appearance of the Maharajah with the fire extinguishers, at the critical moment to save Ludo's home and yoga studio. If someone had summoned him, his timely appearance would make more sense.

Only yesterday, Sid had been at pains to give her his business card, and when he did, she had seen that it provided contact details but no name.

Finally, there was the reaction of the staff member a short while earlier, when she told him she had come to see Sid.

The feelings she had found in herself for Sid and his thoughtfulness and compassion for her had seemed real enough. But why all the mystery?

There was the sound of footsteps descending the staircase, and then Sid strode across the hallway in our direction. He came to a sudden halt when he stepped into the reception room and found Serena in front of the family photographs.

"So, *you're* the Maharajah." Her tone was more surprised than accusing.

His expression solemn, he nodded once.

"So why . . . ?"

"At a very great cost I have learned the importance of discretion. I was planning to tell you directly, Serena. I didn't expect you to come here like this."

"Evidently."

He gestured to a chair. "Please let me explain."

Once again, the two of them sat facing each other, she in a chair, he on a sofa. Once again, I sniffed the legs of the furniture, this time examining the curtains and ornate Indian carpets with intense curiosity. Here, too, everything seemed powerfully familiar.

Even familial.

"My grandfather inherited a vast estate when he was my age," Sid was telling Serena. "Even by the opulent standards of the imperial maharajahs, he was a very, very wealthy man. His diamonds were counted by the pound, his pearls measured by the acre, his gold bars by the ton.

"He also inherited a staff of over ten thousand, including forty concubines and their children, and over one thousand bodyguards. There were twenty people whose sole occupation was to collect drinking water for the extended family from the nearest well, some miles away."

Serena was listening with rapt attention. I jumped on the sofa and sidled over toward Sid, testing one of his legs with my right paw. When he made no objection, I climbed onto his lap, circled a few times to find the best position, then settled on his pinstriped trousers. Once I did, he stroked me reassuringly. It was as though we had sat together like this many times in the past.

"Unfortunately," Sid continued, "unlike our predecessors, my grandfather was not an astute man. Everyone took advantage of him: his advisers, his servants, even his so-called friends. Over the years he lost all his estates and money. I remember my father taking me to visit him on his deathbed. By that time the palace was ramshackle, stripped of most of its valuables, but even then it was overrun with people who had supposedly come to pay their respects. My father had a firm of private bodyguards put at the gates to search everyone on their way out." Sid shook his head. "I can't begin to describe the 'souvenirs' they found people trying to steal.

"By the time my father became Maharajah, it was a title with very little else, except for a decaying building in the foothills of the Himalayas to which he never returned. He had little interest in commerce and devoted himself to spiritual pursuits instead. He leaned toward Buddhism, which is why he named me Siddhartha, after the Buddha's birth name."

I purred.

"Perhaps because he was so unworldly, my father didn't realize what the loss of the family fortune actually meant. We still lived as though we had money, and there were always willing creditors because of the family name. He sent me abroad to be educated, and I got involved with a girl who was also under the illusion she was marrying an heir.

"When the creditors finally lost their patience with my father and began threatening him, he died of a heart attack. My girlfriend left me. I came home to a grieving mother and a mountain of debt. So you see"—Sid met Serena's eyes with a penetrating expression—"since then I have been very reluctant to use a title and family name that have been so . . . problematic."

Serena looked at him with compassion. "I'm very sorry to hear all that," she said warmly. "How awful for you."

"It's in the past." He nodded briskly. "Since then I have enjoyed some success in business. Unlike my ancestors, I have focused on benefiting the community, as well as myself. That is why I am interested in, for example, fair-trade spices."

She smiled. "You're being too modest." With a gesture that encompassed the building and surrounding gardens, she said, "It seems to me you've been *very* successful. That must make you happy."

Sid considered this for a long time before saying, "I think it is actually the other way around. Happiness comes first, then success."

As Serena listened closely, he continued. "When I returned to India, I faced many challenges, but in my heart I felt sure of my purpose. I wanted to achieve the balance in my life that both my father and grandfather had lacked. Meditation practice and yoga for mental and physical well-being—of course. Business activities to generate money benefiting self and others—yes, that too. It didn't matter so much that I lived and worked in a tiny, two-bedroom place right above the market. I already felt part of the community. In small ways I was able to help. When you have that contentment within, whether or not you achieve your goals, I think success becomes more likely."

"The paradox of nonattachment," agreed Serena.

"Not many people would understand."

Serena held his gaze for a long time before gesturing to the painting on the wall. "Is that your family home?"

Sid nodded. "A painting from my grandfather's era. It's still much the same, but slowly, slowly we are restoring it to some of its former glory."

"It's magnificent!"

"The Palace of the Four Pavilions. In its day, it was sublime. These days, it's only just habitable. My mother moved there a year ago from Delhi, along with her family of Himalayan cats. Just like this one."

I looked up inquiringly at Sid.

Delhi. Where I was born. To the cat of a family believed to be wealthy, who had moved soon afterward, and no one had been able to trace.

"You look very at home with her on your lap."

"Oh, yes. They are very special creatures, especially sensitive to people's mood and energy." Then after a moment he asked, "So am I correct in thinking we may be able to work together introducing the world to spice packs?"

For a while they talked about distribution, supply chains, online marketing, and celebrity endorsements. But I could sense that beneath it all, something else was happening. That afternoon, with the sun's rays reaching through the bay window, it was as though Sid and Serena were dancing.

Then it was time for Serena to go and get ready for yoga. As we left the room, she turned, looking back at the painting. "I would love to see the Palace of the Four Pavilions. Would you take me there one day?"

Sid smiled broadly. "It would be my great pleasure."

The three of us made our way to the door. Sid stood at the top of the steps and watched us go.

Partway down the path, Serena turned around. "By the way . . . *Siddartha*," she said, shielding her eyes from the afternoon sun, "the night of the fire: my scarf *was* on the balcony, wasn't it?"

There was a long pause before he nodded.

A late afternoon breeze carried with it the sultry promise of evening jasmine. Serena kissed the tips of her fingers and blew the kiss to Sid.

With a smile, he brought his palms together at his heart.

CHAPTER ELEVEN

The day of His Holiness's return finally arrived! Waking from my 44th sleep alone on the yak blanket, I remembered that the Dalai Lama would be home within hours even before I opened my eyes. I hopped off the bed with glee.

From early that morning, the whole of Jokhang was abuzz with preparations. From His Holiness's study came the sounds of cleaners giving the place a final dust and vacuum. When I emerged from our apartment, having had a few mouthfuls of breakfast, fresh flowers were being delivered and placed in the reception areas, to welcome not only the Dalai Lama but also the many guests he would soon be receiving.

In the executive assistants' office, Tenzin's chair was empty. He and the driver were on their way to Kangra Airport to meet His Holiness as he got off the plane. On the way back, Tenzin would brief the Dalai Lama on the most urgent and important matters requiring his attention.

Across the desk, Yogi Tarchin had no sooner finished speaking to one person than another was making further demands. Far from showing any sign of irritation, he was easy, even playful, in the way he dealt with it all. A lightness pervaded the room.

That feeling was not, alas, in evidence somewhat farther down the corridor when I paused at Lobsang's door. His typically serene presence was curiously altered. For a while I watched as he tidied his shelves, sorted through a number of files before placing several neatly on his desk, and glanced about his office in a distracted manner. It was a while before I realized what he seemed to be feeling: it was apprehension.

No such concerns troubled others at Jokhang. Instead there was a celebratory frisson in the air. His Holiness would soon be back among us, and with him our whole purpose for being here would return. A flurry of couriers arrived bearing gifts, parcels, and important correspondence. In the staff room voices were raised with urgency, and laughter echoed down the hallway as people discovered fresh meaning in their work. From the kitchen came the unmistakable aromas of Mrs. Trinci's cooking, as she prepared lunch for His Holiness's first visitors.

As a cat with well-developed feline intuition, I knew exactly when the Dalai Lama would be getting home. So instead of lounging on the filing cabinet in the executive assistants' office, I opted for my favorite spot when His Holiness was in residence—the windowsill of the main reception room. It was here that he spent so much of his time, and here that I eavesdropped on the most intriguing conversations. And, of top priority to a cat, it was here that I could observe all the comings and goings in the courtyard below.

Not every single coming or going was *closely* observed. After all, what's the point of breakfast if it isn't followed by a postprandial nap? Not to mention that the gentle breeze blowing through the open window had the most delightfully soporific effect. So a short while later, I was roused by the sound of applause coming from the corridor outside. The door of the reception room opened, and the security men made a final check. Suddenly His Holiness appeared.

He entered the room and looked directly at me. The instant our eyes met, I was suffused with happiness so great it was almost overwhelming. Leaving his entourage of staff and advisers behind, he came straight over and lifted me into his arms.

"How are you, my little Snow Lion?" he murmured. "I have missed you!"

He turned so that together we were looking out the window and down Kangra Valley. In that Himalaya morning it seemed as though the air had never been so crisp, the sky never so clear, the scent of cypress and rhododendron never so strong. Gazing down at the stone paths cushioned with pine needles, I was in wordless communication with His Holiness.

As I purred, he chuckled softly, recollecting our last conversation before he left. Did he even need to ask if I had explored the art of purring?

He did not.

Nor did I have to tell him, because he knew my experiences with greater clarity and compassion than I did myself. The Dalai Lama was well aware of what I had learned during his time away. He knew that in listening to the famous psychologist down at the Himalaya Book Café I had come to realize that despite all our ideas about what will make us happy, much of the time our expectations are wrong. He knew, too, that Viktor Frankl's observation that happiness arises as a side effect of one's dedication to a cause greater than oneself was resonant with meaning for me.

From Ludo at the yoga studio, I had discovered that happiness isn't to be found in the past. Gordon Finlay had proven that it shouldn't be expected in some mythical future either. And if I was to learn anything from Chogyal's early death, it was that only by developing a keen sense of life's evanescence would I be able to experience each day for what it is—a miracle.

Sam Goldberg and his Happiness Formula had convinced me that whatever our circumstances or temperament, each of us has the capacity for greater happiness through practices like meditation. Not to mention that when we help others, we ourselves are often the first beneficiaries. Could there be a better reason to purr?

Through Namgyal Monastery's disciplinarian I had come to understand how often mood is linked to food. And the personal crises faced by Serena and Sam that had prompted one of Geshe Wangpo's surprise interventions had served as a practical lesson in how to cultivate equanimity.

Siddhartha, the Maharajah of Himachal Pradesh seemed to be living proof that the relationship between happiness and success is the reverse of what many people assume.

But it was Yogi Tarchin who had made me see what a limited view I had of my own mind as well as my potential for happiness. And the British biologist had offered hope to all us *sem chens* in explaining that the capacity for panoramic understanding is something possessed by all sentient beings. What a breathtaking shift occurs when we see ourselves as consciousness capable of human, feline, or even canine experiences, rather than as people, cats, or dogs capable of conscious experience.

The Dalai Lama and I shared our understanding of all this as we enjoyed the Himalaya morning together. And, as he had promised before leaving on his trip, the moment had arrived for him to share his thoughts about the true causes of happiness—to pass on the message intended specifically for me and for those with whom I have a karmic connection. Since you have stayed with me for this long, dear reader, that includes you!

"There is a special wisdom about happiness," His Holiness told me. "Some texts call it *the Holy Secret*. Like much wisdom, it is simple to explain but not easy to live. The Holy Secret is this: If you wish to end your suffering, seek to end the suffering of others. If you wish for happiness, seek the happiness of others. Exchanging thoughts of self for thoughts of others—*this* is the most effective way to be happy."

I absorbed the significance of his words along with the morning air blowing through the open window. The idea of thinking about others nearly as much as I thought about myself was, indeed, challenging. HHC, the Snow Lion, Rinpoche, Swami, the Most Beautiful Creature That Ever Lived—it is she who is at the center of my consciousness from the moment I wake every morning until I go to sleep at night.

"Thinking too much about oneself is a cause of much suffering," the Dalai Lama said. "Anxiety, depression, resentment, fear—these become much worse with too much attention to the self. The mantra *Me, me, me* is not so good."

Now that he had pointed it out, I realized that the times when I had been the unhappiest were the times when I had been the most preoccupied with myself. When I became angry with Chogyal for ordering the cleaning of my blanket, for example, no one else's happiness had been in my thoughts at that moment—certainly not Chogyal's!

And then there was another all-important teaching His Holiness imparted: "It is not necessary to end the suffering of all beings in order to end your own suffering, or for all beings to be happy in order for you to be happy. If that were the case," he said with a chuckle, "then all Buddhas would have failed!

"We can all learn to use this marvelous paradox," he told me, looking deep into my sapphire blue eyes. "Be wisely selfish, little Snow Lion. Gain happiness for yourself by giving it to others." He was silent for a moment, stroking my face with exquisite tenderness. "You do this already, I think, each time you purr."

His Holiness's return was more than enough excitement for one day. But things were to get even better. Because high-level delegates from the United Nations were staying for lunch, I would be able to visit Mrs. Trinci in the kitchen. And true to form, she rewarded my visit with a reminder of my incomparable beauty, as well as a generous portion of succulent shrimp garnished with a goat's cheese sauce. Such was the delicious creaminess of the latter that it took me quite a while to lick the saucer clean.

Afterward, I sat in the dappled afternoon sunshine outside the kitchen, washing my face, feeling replete and contented. His Holiness was back in residence. Mrs. Trinci would, once again, be a regular visitor. All was as it should be in my world.

And there was something else to look forward to: a short ceremony that evening to mark the reopening of the balcony at the Downward Dog School of Yoga. In recent days, the front of Ludo's house had been teeming with workmen replacing fire-damaged beams with more robust steel supports. I had heard Serena speak with enthusiasm about the newly refurbished balcony, which was stronger and wider than the one before and furnished with a beautiful hand-woven carpet given to Ludo by his students. As the balcony had yet to be used, Ludo had decided to mark the occasion with an official rededication, to be presided over by a mystery guest.

Moving in the rarefied circles I do, dear reader, I knew exactly who the mystery guest was to be. And as one of my intimates, I'm sure you have a pretty good idea, too. Since the occasion would find so many of my favorite people gathered under one roof, I decided that I, the Swami of the Downward Dog School of Yoga, should be in attendance.

I began making my way up Bougainvillea Street in the late afternoon, passing the spice shop that had been the scene of such panic and mayhem some weeks ago. I walked along the stretch of sidewalk where I had felt so trapped. And it was as I was walking by the high, white wall of Sid's property that it happened—again. The same two canine monsters appeared from nowhere, charging directly toward me. Only this time was different. Worse. There was no possibility of escape.

A more robust cat might have darted across the road, scaled a wall, and made good its escape. But I knew my limitations. There was no way out.

I turned toward my pursuers and, at the very moment they reached me, sat down. My action caught them totally by surprise as they romped toward me, in anticipation of a hot pursuit. They shoved their paws out in front and came to a scrambling halt. As they towered over me, I was enveloped in hot and sulphorous panting. Tongues lolling and saliva dribbling from their mouths, they thrust their noses toward me.

What did I do? I snarled. Opening my mouth as wide as possible, I hissed with the fury of a wrathful deity a thousand times their size. My heart was thundering, my hair was standing on end. But as I bared my fangs and whipped my mouth back and forth from left to right, the two great beasts pulled back, cocking their heads in surprise.

This was not the reception they had expected. Nor one they particularly liked. One of the monsters drove his snout to within an inch of my face. Like a flash of lightning I lashed out with my paw in stinging rebuke. The beast let out a high-pitched yelp, abruptly pulling back in pain.

We were at a stalemate. They had cornered me— something they hadn't exactly planned. And now that it had happened, they didn't know what to do. My display of ferocity had thrown them completely off their game.

Just in time, the tall man in the tweed jacket arrived. "Come on, you two," he called out in a jocular tone.

"Leave that poor cat alone." They seemed only too relieved to be put back on their leashes and led away.

Watching them go, I found, to my great surprise, that I was a lot less traumatized by the encounter than I had expected. I had faced down my worst fear and discovered I could cope. I was stronger than I thought. It had been a testing experience, but I had successfully held my own against the two slavering hounds.

As I continued on my way, I recollected something His Holiness had told me—that thinking too much about oneself is a cause of suffering and that fear and anxiety become worse when we focus on *me.* Suddenly I wondered if I had ended up smeared with spices and trapped on the wall all those weeks ago not because of the dogs but rather because I had focused on nothing but saving my own fur. Would I have fared better if I had stood my ground and stared down my pursuers? Could so-called self-preservation sometimes backfire and become the very cause of pain?

Having fought off the two beasts, I felt more robust and assured as I continued up the hill. I might be one small, somewhat crippled cat, but I had the heart of a Snow Lion! I had confounded my shadows. I was Swami, Vanquisher of Golden Retrievers!

Ludo's house was looking festive for the occasion. A new display of vividly colored Tibetan prayer flags fluttered under the eaves, carrying countless prayers on the wind. The hallway had been redecorated and smelled of fresh paint. *The Downward Dog School of Yoga* had been restenciled over the entrance.

The studio was packed with more people than I'd ever seen there before. All the regular yogis and yoginis were there, including Merrilee—sans hipflask—Jordan, and Ewing, while many of the others looked as though they had never seen the inside of a yoga studio before but were intrigued by the promise of Ludo's mystery guest. I recognized patrons of the café and McLeod Ganj locals I had passed in the street—even Ludo's next-door neighbors, in whose house the fire had started. As I picked my way through the rows of yoga mats to my usual spot, my arrival was duly noted.

I was glad to find one person in the back row who, although out of context, was warmly familiar. It was Lobsang, and the moment I saw him, I thought how relieved he looked. Sitting quietly on his own, he was a monk unburdened. His serenity had returned, and as he reached out to stroke me, his eyes were filled with peace.

At the front of the room, the sliding doors were wide open, revealing the spectacular vista of the Himalayas. The new balcony lay behind a ribbon of four interwoven colors—blue, green, red, and gold—that stirred gently in the late afternoon, ready to be cut in the official opening ceremony.

There was a bustle of activity at the door, then Serena arrived. Looking around, she spotted Lobsang alone in the back and immediately came over to him.

"How did it go?" she whispered, sitting down and reaching over to touch his arm.

He smiled and nodded. He seemed to be finding it hard to speak.

Serena's expression was warm. "You're okay, then?"

"I didn't even need to ask him," he eventually managed to say. "When I went to see him, he spent a few minutes telling me how much he liked my work on the new book. Then he looked directly at me and said, 'You are still a young man, with many talents. Perhaps it would be a good idea to try something new, if you like.'"

"Oh, Lobsang," she said, turning to hug him.

"I finish in six weeks," he told her, his mouth curled with emotion. "After that, I am free to travel."

"Have you thought about where?"

"His Holiness has offered me an introduction to the abbot of a monastery in Thailand." His eyes flickered with excitement. "I think my adventures may begin there."

I absorbed what Lobsang was saying with strongly mixed feelings. He had always been a serene presence at Jokhang, and I had taken for granted that he would remain there. I was sad that he was going. But in recent months I had also known that something wasn't quite right. Despite the great value of his work, he had felt restless and in need of a new direction. It was a further reminder that the only constant is change.

Moments later Sam pushed his way through the bead curtain. After taking in the stunning panorama for the first time, he looked around the room. Serena waved, and he came over to join her, followed moments later by Bronnie.

As they sat beside her, Serena took a close look at them. "I'm glad to see you two here together," she said.

"Kathmandu has a lot going for it," murmured Bronnie, "but it doesn't have Sam."

Serena nodded. "So you're staying in India?"

As Bronnie shook her head, Sam cut in. "Three-month contract. Bronnie will be on her own for the first two months. I'll join her for month three. Then we'll both come back here."

"Sounds like a good arrangement," Serena said.

"This way we both get to see more of the Himalayas," explained Bronnie. "Though I think Sam is more interested in checking out the Kopan Monastery bookstore."

"Habit of a lifetime," observed Serena.

"Once a geek . . . ," said Sam.

"*Super*-geek," corrected Bronnie. Reaching over, she took his hand in hers.

Ludo appeared from the hallway and made his way to the front of the studio, leonine and supple as ever. Wearing a white cotton tunic and white yoga pants, he was more smartly dressed than usual but ready to lead what would turn out to be a very gentle yoga session, one intended to introduce newcomers to some of the basics of the practice.

It was while Ludo was explaining *Tadasana,* Mountain Pose, that Sid arrived, uncharacteristically late. He spotted Serena at the back and headed her way. Without being asked, Sam and Bronnie moved over so that he and Serena could sit together.

They were right in front of where I was sitting. I watched them move through a sequence of stretches, balancing on one leg with their arms toward the ceiling, followed by twists, first to the right, then the left. At one point, Serena turned the wrong way by mistake, so that she and Sid were facing each other. Instead of staring at a point in the distance, they met each other's eyes and held the gaze for a minute of unexpected, unwavering intimacy.

Ludo took the class through a handful of seated postures. It was while they were all tucked in *Balasana,* Child's Pose, that two security men appeared. They checked the room then nodded to Ludo, who told everyone to sit up.

Smiling, he said, "I know the real reason that many of you are here. And it is my great privilege and heartfelt pleasure to invite our honored guest, His Holiness, the Fourteenth Dalai Lama of Tibet, to rededicate our yoga studio."

Gasps of happiness greeted the announcement. As His Holiness appeared in the hallway, out of respect everyone started to stand, but he waved them to stay as they were. "Please, sit," he said, then brought his palms together at his heart and bowed, as he met the eyes of everyone in the room.

When the Dalai Lama walks to the front of a room full of people, he doesn't walk past them but engages many of them on the way. This evening, as he headed toward Ludo he squeezed Ewing's shoulder and chuckled as he looked into Merrilee's eyes. When Sukie placed her hands together and bowed, he gently reached out and held her hands briefly in his. A tear rolled down her cheek.

By the time His Holiness reached Ludo, who was standing at the front, there was an awed hush in the room. Everyone felt the energy he exuded unceasingly and without effort. It was an energy that could move you beyond your usual limited sense of yourself to an awareness of your boundless nature and the reassuring knowledge that all is well. Pausing in front of the open doors, the Dalai Lama gave himself over to the spectacular view.

The natural elements had conspired to stage an especially transcendent sunset that evening. The deep lapis sky created a dramatic backdrop for glistening peaks that were painted with liquid gold. Immense and immutable as the Himalayas usually seemed, on this occasion they shimmered like an ethereal vision that might dissolve into emptiness at any moment.

As His Holiness stood taking in this vista, his wonderment was communicated to everyone in the studio. For a few timeless moments, we were held together, spellbound. Then he turned to Ludo with a smile.

Ludo bowed formally, offering the Dalai Lama a white scarf in the traditional way. When His Holiness returned the scarf, placing it around Ludo's shoulders, he reached down and took Ludo's hand in his. "My good friend," he began, patting their joined hands. Then, looking out at us, he said, "Many years ago, when I first came to Dharamsala, I heard about this German man who wanted to teach yoga. *This is good,* I thought. *The Germans are very persistent!*"

There was much laughter.

"Mindfulness of the body is a foundation practice. It is most useful. If we want to cultivate mindfulness, yoga can be very helpful. This is why I always say to Ludo, 'Teach more yoga. It will benefit all who come.'"

The Dalai Lama's eyes twinkled behind his glasses as he surveyed the group. "The body is like a treasure chest. The treasure it houses is the mind. The opportunity we have to develop our mind is very, very precious. Most beings have no such opportunity. This is why we should take good care of our bodies and look after our health. Make the most of this lifetime to benefit the self and benefit others."

His Holiness gestured to Ludo to speak. After welcoming the Dalai Lama to the Downward Dog School of Yoga, he explained that the studio was named not only for the yoga pose that was now known around the world but also for a dog he had looked after in his earliest days in

McLeod Ganj. His Holiness wore a contemplative expression as he gazed at the picture of the Lhasa Apso hanging on the studio wall.

Ludo spoke of being encouraged by the Dalai Lama's support from the start. Now, several decades later, he couldn't imagine life without this special purpose, teaching yoga. The recent fire and the restoration of the balcony had presented an opportunity to begin a new chapter for the studio, he said.

Chanting a prayer in Tibetan, the Dalai Lama blessed the studio and every being in it. In that brief moment, the atmosphere in the room seemed to change. As the consciousness of His Holiness touched our own, each of us felt something sacred and profound.

Ludo handed His Holiness a pair of scissors and invited him to cut the ribbon to the new balcony. This he did, to much amusement and applause. Then Ludo said, "I have told His Holiness the story of the fire and how things could have been much worse if it hadn't been for little Swami."

Sitting in front of me, Sid called out, "She's here tonight."

"Is she?"

As Sid and Serena moved aside, all eyes were suddenly upon me. The Dalai Lama looked directly at me with heartfelt love. Then glancing again at the framed photograph of the Lhasa Apso, hanging on the wall he turned to Ludo and said, "I am so pleased she has found her way back to you."

Later that night I lay resting on the yak blanket at the foot of His Holiness's bed while he sat up reading. As I stared up at him, I thought about his comment to Ludo, the photograph on the wall of the yoga studio, and my dream. I also remembered Yogi Tarchin calling me *Little Sister* as soon as he'd seen me with Serena. And I thought about how comfortable and at home I felt with both Serena and Sid.

During these past seven weeks I had come to some life-changing realizations about happiness, but I had also uncovered something else—something as profound and heart-warming as it was completely unexpected. I had discovered the depth of my connection to the people I was closest to, a bond that went far beyond my imagining. I had shared whole lifetimes with them, even though the memory of this wasn't always accessible to me.

The Dalai Lama looked down at me with a smile. Closing his book, he removed his glasses and placed them carefully on the bedside table, then leaned down to stroke my face.

"Yes, little Snow Lion, it is no coincidence that you and I are here. We have created the causes to be together. For my part, I am very, very happy that is so."

For my part, too, I thought, purring appreciatively.

His Holiness turned off the light.

If you liked
The Art of Purring,
check out the first book in this series...

THE
DALAI LAMA'S
CAT

"Oh! How adorable! I didn't know you had a cat!" she exclaimed.

I am always surprised how many people make this observation. Why should His Holiness not have a cat?

"If only she could speak," continued the actress. "I'm sure she'd have such wisdom to share."

And so the seed was planted . . .

I began to think that perhaps the time had come for me to write a book of my own—a book that would convey some of the wisdom I've learned sitting not at the feet of the Dalai Lama but even closer, on his lap. A book that would tell my own tale . . . how I was rescued from a fate too grisly to contemplate to become the constant companion of a man who is not only one of the world's greatest spiritual leaders and a Nobel Peace Prize Laureate but also a dab hand with a can opener."

Starving and pitiful, a mud-smeared kitten is rescued from the slums of New Delhi and transported to a life she could have never imagined. In a beautiful sanctuary overlooking the snow-capped Himalayas, she begins her new life as the Dalai Lama's cat.

Warmhearted, irreverent, and wise, this cat of many names opens a window to the inner sanctum of life in Dharamsala. A tiny spy observing the constant flow of private meetings between His Holiness and everyone from Hollywood celebrities to philanthropists to self-help authors, the Dalai Lama's cat provides us with insights on how to find happiness and meaning in a busy, materialistic world. Her story will put a smile on the face of anyone who has been blessed by the kneading paws and bountiful purring of a cat.

ABOUT THE AUTHOR

 **David Michie** is the bestselling author of *The Dalai Lama's Cat*, *Buddhism for Busy People*, *Hurry Up and Meditate* and *Enlightenment to Go*. All have been published internationally and are being translated into many languages. David was born in Zimbabwe, educated at Rhodes University in South Africa, and lived in London for ten years. He is married and based in Perth, Australia.

www.davidmichie.com

Hay House Titles of Related Interest

YOU CAN HEAL YOUR LIFE, the movie,
starring Louise L. Hay & Friends
(available as a 1-DVD programme and an expanded 2-DVD set)
Watch the trailer at: www.LouiseHayMovie.com

THE SHIFT, the movie,
starring Dr Wayne W. Dyer
(available as a 1-DVD programme and an expanded 2-DVD set)
Watch the trailer at: www.DyerMovie.com

THE DIVINITY OF DOGS:
True Stories of Miracles Inspired by Man's Best Friend,
by Jennifer Skiff

THE FIRST RULE OF TEN: A Tenzing Norbu Mystery,
by Gay Hendricks and Tinker Lindsay

THE LAST LAUGH, by Arjuna Ardagh

THE MAN WHO WANTED TO BE HAPPY,
by Laurent Gounelle

PEOPLE OF THE GREAT JOURNEY,
by O.R. Melling

SMILING THE MOON,
by Tom Lawrence

THE RADICAL PRACTICE OF LOVING EVERYONE:
A Four-Legged Approach to Enlightenment, by Michael J. Chase

All of the above may be ordered at www.hayhouse.co.uk

HAY HOUSE

Look within

Join the conversation about latest products,
events, exclusive offers and more.

 Hay House

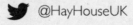 @HayHouseUK

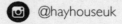 @hayhouseuk

We'd love to hear from you!